MUTLEY

MY STORY, MY WAY!

Bob Lamb

First published in 2024 by Gunner Enterprises

ISBN 978-1-8382488-2-6

Copyright © Bob Lamb, 2024

Edited by Sarah Walker

The right of Bob Lamb to be identified as the author of this work has been asserted in accordance with the Copyright, Designs and Patents Act, 1988.

All rights reserved. No part of this publication may be reproduced, stored in a retrieval system, or transmitted, in any form or by any means (electronic, mechanical, photocopying, recording or otherwise), without the prior written permission of the publisher.

A CIP catalogue record for this book is available from the British Library.

Printed and bound by IngramSpark.

Cover image created by Sarah Walker with WIX AI Image Creator

Typesetting by Sarah Walker via IngramSpark

In memory of Gunner,

1985 ~ 2005

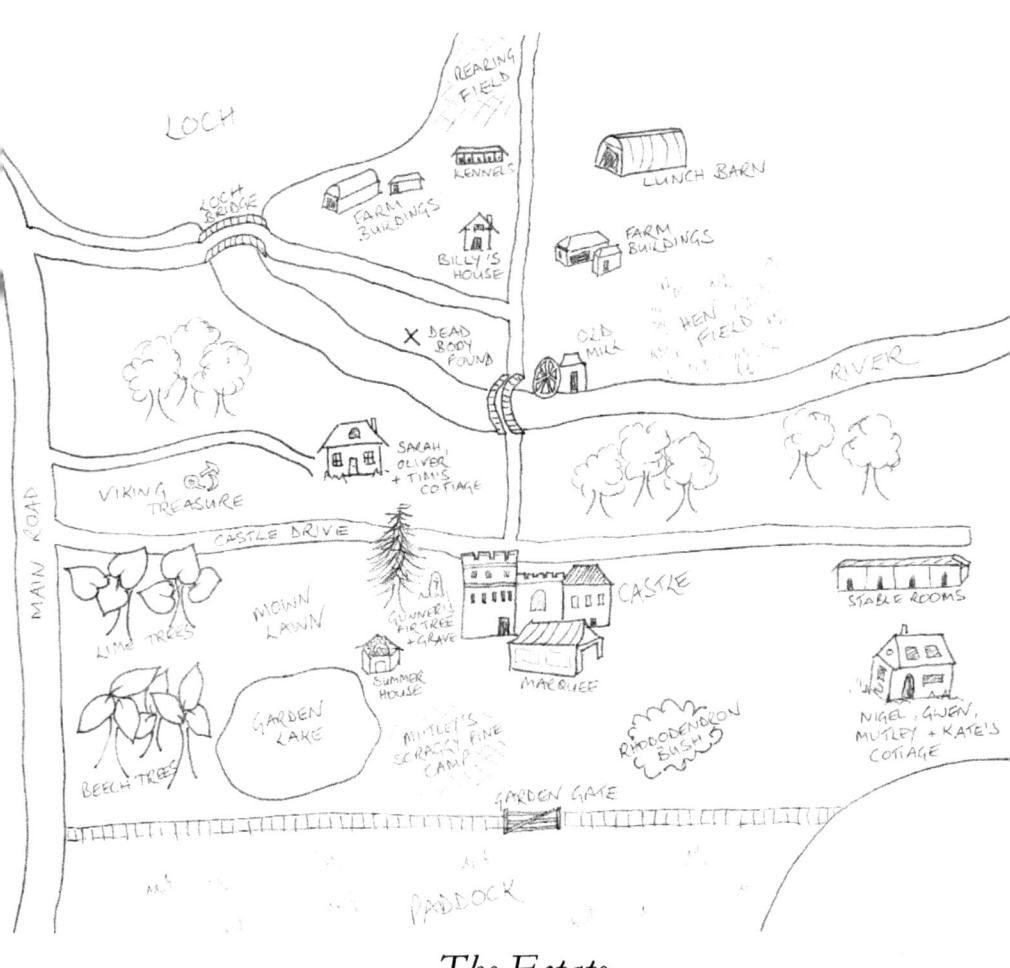

The Estate

Main Characters

Nigel, *the laird*

🐾 **Mutley**, *a handsome Sprocker and the narrator*

Gwen, *the housekeeper and Nigel's girlfriend*

Oliver, *the farm manager and Nigel's brother*

Sarah, *Oliver's wife and events caterer*

Tim, *Sarah and Oliver's son*

Ian, *the castle manager*

Jane, *the assistant manager*

Billy, *the gamekeeper*

🐾 **Bill**, *a black Labrador*

Freddie, *Billy's assistant*

🐾 **Jock**, *an old, fat Labrador*

The Body, *a shoot guest*

🐾 **Ben**, *a good but very sad Labrador*

Joe, *an old friend*

🐾 **Kate**, *a Spaniel with special gifts*

Peter, *the handyman*

PROLOGUE

If a story spans a year, is it a diary? Possibly! Though this is no ordinary story during a very unordinary year, and I am no ordinary dog.

While I am, for the most part, a modest dog and rarely vain, everyone tells me I'm very handsome. My father was a tall, dark Cocker Spaniel who often told of his prowess in the show ring. Mother was a liver and white Springer Spaniel. I am, therefore, what many would call a 'Sprocker'! When father was there, she let him hold court about how he had been the best dog in the ring and would have won Crufts, if only the judges had been up to it.

But when he was away, and my brothers, sisters and I were all curled up and nearly asleep, mother would tell us tales of being up on the hill or in the deep woods, or out as the moon came up and the duck flew into feed. These were the stories I loved then, and still remember now.

I am five years old - in my prime, some would say – with a passion for hunting: nose to the ground, through every bit of rough cover. I stand just forty centimetres tall on my four (seldom clean) paws and my life may not be as yours, but I am proud of it and look forward to sharing it with you.

1

The festivities are over, and the guests have gone; they have exhausted me! I breathe deeply, stretch out a paw and close my eyes. Some may think I'm sleeping, escaping this second day of a New Year, but I'm not. I'm fully aware that Nigel is running from the gorgeous Gwen, and Oliver, Nigel's brother, is running from everyone.

My home is a Scottish castle. Its huge front door creaks open, a chill wind penetrates my fur, and I give up hope of rest. Gwen and Oliver walk outside, and I follow them. Both speak to me - they often do. They seem to think that because I'm a dog, they don't have to hide what they really think or say. Humans!

The frozen snow crackles under their feet, and Gwen shivers. Scents seem different this morning, so I lick the snow to clear my head and it tastes good!

Oliver has returned indoors. I heard him stamping snow from his feet, and he's now with Nigel in the office. Its window is crazed with frost, but I can see their faces through it and know Gwen is looking at them too. I want Oliver to smile, to let me know what he's hiding, what's worrying him. But he looks away as Nigel turns, comes outside and puts his coat in the Land Rover. Hurrah! I picture us bouncing up the valley and into a wood – which one will it be? Yet I know Gwen also wants him, she wants to go shopping.

Nigel looks at me and calls, 'Mutley!'

I leap through the opened back door of the vehicle; my feet slide on the old sack that covers the floor and my tail wags uncontrollably as I press my nose against the dirty window. I am suddenly happy as the glass steams up and an angry Gwen disappears behind it.

We drive up a frozen track and stop in a gateway where a wood meets the track and a field shows the way up the hill. Why are we here? Is there work for me or does Nigel just want to escape from Gwen and the shopping?

Nigel wipes snow from a bird feeder and, as he taps it, golden grain flows onto the untouched snow. The snow has blown from much of the field and lies in heaps against the fence and trees. The valley below looks very cold and very wet; much of the bottom ground is frozen, and in places snow has settled on the ice. I think how difficult it would be to find anything with so much water and so much ice…but so much fun!

And yet, as I look, something wants to spoil my view, but before I can creep away to see Nigel strokes me as he only does when he's worried - when whatever is buzzing around in his head can't find anywhere to land. He smiles, as if my contribution has been vital, and leaps back into the driver's seat. Our trip is over, the shopping is avoided, and the castle beckons.

Nigel walks indoors but I stay by the front door and look out onto the driveway that runs up to the road. Beside it is the lawn and beyond it is the lake. Sometimes the estate is busy - very busy! - but now it is not. The New Year revellers have gone, and everything is quiet.

I move onto the lawn, where the morning sun is glistening on the icy snow and rest under a tree. It's a special tree, a young cedar (or so Nigel tells me) and its dark green, spikey leaves trail right down to the ground. These have been running the ice-cold sleet and snow onto the sleeping grass, leaving my patch dry and warm and, most importantly, invisible. Although I can't be seen, I have a good view of the castle and can spot anyone arriving, which is extremely important!

We are hosting a sporting party tomorrow and I am very excited. Bill, the black Labrador who lives with Billy the gamekeeper, has filled me in on what we will be doing and, after too many days of gentle entertaining, I'm raring to go! Nigel has driven up the track to the farm and I know that he'll be going over the details with Billy for the tenth time. I can picture them all. Nigel talking earnestly with Billy; Oliver's wife, Sarah, at the lunch barn, making ready; everyone in the castle preparing beds and cleaning. In many ways, just another day; each person a cog in the wheel.

I rub an itch on my nose and try to settle into my warm bed of pine needles, but expectancy is in the air, and I can't rest. Sarah returns to the castle from her little house opposite, in a hurry as usual. Ian, the castle manager, and Jane, his assistant, are already there, even though no guests are present, not one.

Although we won't return to the valley until tomorrow, the guests are arriving today. How do I know this, you may ask? I have learnt to know what people say and think, and to understand their words. As with my fellow dogs, I can talk through my eyes and my body. Ask any dog a question and, with some practice, you will understand their answer!

Jane comes outside and picks up a tiny piece of paper that has settled on the mucky ice. Her eyes are distant, and her face looks tired. Ian stands as tall as he can, wanting to look important. He sees another piece of paper, but instead of picking it up himself, he simply points it out to Jane. I rush forward and beat her to it, shaking it in my mouth with mock anger, then run away, ignoring Ian's rebukes, back to my pine bed.

In the middle of the afternoon, five big cars arrive and draw up in front of the castle, waking me as they crunch loudly on the frozen gravel. I must crawl a little to see them, and an odd drip of ice-cold water lands on my nose. I count seven, no, eight men, three women and at least six big, black dogs. I would much rather they were Spaniels, but otherwise these guests look happy enough. There is a mountain of bags and kit, which Ian and Jane help unload. I move from my warm lair to welcome our guests and shiver a little as I do.

The night has come and gone and the party that arrived yesterday is eating breakfast. Their dogs, having enjoyed the freedom of my lawn, are resting. They are some of the most overweight and pompous dogs I have encountered for a long time. I only met them briefly yesterday and when I introduced myself this morning, they looked down their noses at me.

I should not be surprised - after all, they are Retrievers. Ask any Spaniel and he will rarely have a good word for one. They think themselves the glory boys of the sporting field, always looking for an easy life, and if anyone suggests they could put in more effort, they just roll their big, sad eyes as if to say,

'You don't really expect me to go through that nasty, prickly bush, do you?'

Eventually, breakfast completed, the vehicles are loaded, and we are ready for the day. As host, I know I will have to be on my best behaviour, and best behaviour is not really me! I sit on my old sack in the back of the Land Rover and listen to the distant murmuring of Nigel giving instructions.

He comes into view, rubbing his brow, followed by an unhappy looking Billy. Bill is by him, as usual, but – what's this? – so is a strange black dog, pulling on a lead. I have never seen this second dog. Why hasn't Bill told me? Who is he?

The beaters tap their sticks, birds fly and guns fire, until Billy blows his whistle and peace returns. I want to find the birds that are down but must watch whilst those lumbering black beasts sniff slowly. One, a big dog called Brutus, is within a metre of a pheasant, but it sidesteps him and runs up a steep slope. He just watches it go and jogs back to his master as if nothing has happened.

The guests finally accept they can't find the birds and a real dog must do it. The scent has become weak, but under the trees it's held in the damp air, and I find them - even an old cock bird that had crept well up the next hedge. I try not to look superior; it can be so hard being a modest host!

As the day is finishing, the weather turns for the worse and the light starts to fade. A cold east wind brings flurries of snow that sting my eyes and annoy my ears. The guests hurry into an old stone building with a huge roaring fire, for tea and tasty looking biscuits. They used the same building at lunch time and the smell of rich beef stew still lingers in my memory.

Nigel has taken me beside the little burn that runs up the valley. He has asked me to find a bird that one of the guests, an old major, is looking for. I saw the shot myself and know the major totally missed, and I tell Nigel this by giving the ground a cursory look and returning to him for new instructions. He knows I'm right, but the major is adamant, so I have to keep going up and down, through every bush and criss-crossing the very cold water.

In the end, insult is added to injury when the wretched guest insists that a proper, purebred dog be called. Billy has come to help, and I expect him to send Bill, but instead he releases the new dog. He's a Labrador, but smaller than Bill, and (for his breed) he makes a fair go of searching the area. Then he returns and sits by Billy, whispering nervously to me,

'You are right, there is no bird here.'

Eventually, the major walks away, cursing the scent and the dogs; in fact, everything but himself. Nigel pats me and leads the way to the lunch barn, his presence overdue. I hang back and see the new dog wants to join me, but Billy calls him angrily and he scurries off.

The flooded valley is below and, as I gaze down at it, something niggles like a strong scent that won't go away. I jog there, knowing I don't have long, and straight away I am blinded by the sleet and snow bouncing on the icy water. So much water and ice, and so little time, but I find myself hunting to the right. The scent grows, of a pheasant, but not a pheasant! Snow has settled in the sheltered hollows and the water has ice at the edge. It's where the ice meets water that I find it -

The body of a man, dressed in a sporting suit. In his hand, still firmly clasped, is a dead pheasant. Where the ice touches his body, it glistens weakly.

What should I do? I touch him with my nose, but he is cold and stiff. I turn away and race to the barn. I must tell Nigel!

The police arrive and fence off the area. They talk to everyone and take the body away. As it will soon be very dark, I don't know what more they can do.

In the morning, after talking to the police again, yesterday's party begin to leave, and I sigh with relief. I find these formal days difficult - they're not me - and yesterday was especially hard. During the night, the memory of my find kept coming back to me. Who was he? How did he die? How did he get there?

The party were shocked, and then excited, especially when they knew the body wasn't one of them.

'Who was it?', they asked, and were disappointed when nobody could tell them. Still, at least it had given them something to talk about as they noisily ate their supper.

The snow has now been replaced by sheets of ice-cold rain. It's just what I need. As the last guests drive away, I stand by the garden lake and watch the fallen leaves picked up by the breeze. I turn my nose into it, my ears blow back onto my neck, and the stress of yesterday is carried away. I think of walking behind the lake to look for rabbits, but a car comes down the drive and, tempted by who might be in it, I trot back towards the castle.

As I am inspecting my lawn, a young boy appears from behind the drooping branches of a lime tree. He runs towards me, calling. It's Tim and I am overjoyed. Normally he's at school and I wonder why he isn't there now.

After a short play, he shouts, 'I'll see you later!' and disappears over the drive into his garden. I say 'his' garden because it is. He is the son of Sarah and Oliver and that's where he lives.

Sarah appears and calls me as she walks from her house. She likes to make a fuss of me and today I need a fuss - and I sense, so does she. She is very down, like a covey of partridge on a wet morning. Everything seems a struggle, except fussing me! I want to ask her why Tim's at home and why she is so down but see this is not the time. We cross the drive to the castle, through the slush that is forming into large puddles, and are soon by the main desk. Ian stands as we arrive.

A police car parks outside and its occupants enter the castle. They are the same ones who came up the valley yesterday after I showed Nigel my find. They must have come to talk to him again, though he knows very little. He doesn't even know the body had a dead pheasant in its hand, and how could he? I didn't tell him. I retrieved it myself and put it with the rest of the day's bag. A good bird should not be wasted!

I think back on the simple bits of the day, which seem to matter more than ever. The last of the sporting guests to leave had been named Pete. He had chatted solemnly to Nigel before slowly lifting his old, stiff dog, Brutus, into the back of his car.

'Could you ever have jumped up?', I asked myself, and doubted it.

A short time later, I look up from my leather sofa to see a young couple standing nervously. Weddings are best in the summer, but planning starts now, and these people seem in need of it. Ian explodes into a man of infinite welcome and whisks them into the oak-panelled sitting room with its roaring fire, to launch his charm offensive.

I look at Sarah. I try to give her a reassuring smile and feel my lips roll back over my teeth, but this makes her hide her face behind her hands and I see tears roll down her cheeks. I lie on her feet to comfort her. Why is she so sad?

She looks at me and smiles a wet smile, then gets up and leaves. She doesn't want anyone to see that she is crying, and I'm pleased I didn't count as anyone. The phone rings, and Ian comes running, calling for Sarah. I'm needed, I can see, and jog through to take over where Ian has left off.

The girl is facing the fireplace. As I approach, she turns and looks down on me, her eyes peering through puffy cheeks with a mixture of surprise and annoyance. I turn, walk away and hop back onto my sofa. Snuggling down, I can hear the clinking of cups in the sitting room, the crackle of the fire and the warmth of Jane's voice.

These comfortable sounds could easily have driven me to sleep, but I can't relax. Is it stiffness after a busy day up the valley, or the lingering shock of finding my body? I shuffle a little, as if this small movement might drive away the discomfort. I close my eyes tight and then open them, but it's still there.

I resort to my cedar tree. My mind wants to think of the valley and everything that matters there, yet the body just won't go away! It was wrong when I first saw it and is just as wrong now. I try to sleep, but the face stares at me - the face of the body that had been a man. I try to picture his eyes, to piece together the question I know he wants to ask me, but it won't come into focus.

One day I will find the question and answer it!

2

A week has passed, and thoughts of the body still fill my head. I have tried extra rabbit hunting and been to Sarah's house several times in the hope of seeing Tim, but he hasn't been there. Our next sporting day has now arrived - I hope I don't find any more bodies!

It's a real January day, crisp and bright. Nigel's Land Rover crunches down the drive and I race to meet him. Again, Billy is there with the new dog. Bill told me that he just turned up from nowhere and that Fred, Billy's assistant, found him very cold and hungry on the top road. I want to know more and stand beside Nigel, springing up with excitement (and to escape the cold gravel that's chilling my feet), but he is focused on the day, so I will have to wait.

Nigel strides past me and into the castle, but he soon comes out and he isn't smiling. He trips over me and snaps. I know he wants to hold more sporting days before the end of the season, but the hordes of policemen and vehicles have churned up the valley since I discovered the body.

I wait to be asked, for someone to want to know what I saw, but even Nigel only gives me a sad stroke, which solves nothing! We drive up the valley to an area well away from where I found the body; well away from where the policemen and their big dogs with huge feet trampled, and shiny tape still blows in the wind. I look at Nigel as we take a bend too fast, and I'm thrown off my feet. He is certainly in a bad mood today, so I will keep my head down!

When we arrive, I feel better. This is my place. The snow sparkles, the sun is shining and I'm happy, even though sunshine is not good on a sporting day. Guests, who only want a day out, think it's great, but we dogs hate it. The birds don't like flying and if they do happen to take off, they land as soon as possible.

A pheasant walks out from the wood up ahead and starts to walk towards me as if I wasn't there. Perhaps he thinks I'm a sheep dog - which, I have decided, pheasants don't think are dogs at all! At last, he hears the men behind him and decides he should fly, but after a few wing flaps, he just glides down the hill, hugging the ground. Along the line more birds behave the same, flying low, put off by the sun.

I am sitting at Nigel's feet, sucking mud from my paws and hoping no more birds glide past us. I have hosted these guests before - they come several times a season but don't stay with us at the castle. Billy is angry because they are poor shots and moan a lot but, thankfully, today is their last day. Eventually, everyone stops moaning and they go into the lunch barn for an end of season meal. I can hear them clearly from my spot by the door.

They are all talking about the body. Everyone has a theory on who it might have been and what might have happened, but still, no one actually knows. At least, no one has told me, and I am normally the first to know these things. They give Billy a bottle of whisky and Hamish, their team captain, makes a speech.

A short time later, Bill and I are in the Land Rover, lying on the old sack. Apart from the bright sun, it's been a good day, and this is the best bit. Bill and I can rest and talk and enjoy our memories, while Billy and Nigel need to smile, tell the guests what good shots they are and how much better it will all be next year.

I want to discuss the body with someone, someone who will understand, but decide this isn't Bill. Instead, I ask about the new dog, and he is full of it!

'He's very quiet. He won't even speak to me, and when Billy comes near, he just shakes with fear.'

'Do you know where he came from? Does he have a collar?' I ask.

'No, he doesn't, so he must be one of us.' (We working dogs don't wear collars, as you may know, in case they catch on a fence or tree.)

I nod in agreement and decide he must have been lost from a neighbouring estate. That means someone will come looking for him soon enough, unless…? My mind is still on the body, and the strange dog appearing at the same time as my discovery seems too much of a coincidence. I must find a way of talking with this new dog. It might answer a lot of questions!

We arrive home and I see that the lights are shining in Sarah's kitchen. But as I jump down from the warmth of my sack, she comes running past and into the castle through the rain, which has started to fall heavily again. I think she's been crying, but she's so wet with the rain I'm not sure. I lead her to my sofa and persuade her to sit with me. We smile at each other through wet eyes, as she dries me with an old towel. She doesn't tell me why she's unhappy, yet I know she will when she's ready.

The phone rings. Ian returns to answer it and Sarah hurries on her way. I look at Ian as he talks. He is miles away and, but for him, the building is silent. I move from my comfortable nest, nose open the door and follow after Sarah.

As I arrive, Oliver is leaving the cottage and I slip into the kitchen, where Sarah is reading to Tim. They don't notice me, and I curl up quietly in the corner. Tim tries to repeat the words his mother has just read, but he stumbles. I have heard him read before and this is not the same Tim. He stops, and

Sarah puts her arm around him, whispers something and gives him an encouraging smile. He smiles back and continues.

When he finishes, she hugs him, and I decide it's time to emerge. I do so with a yap of praise, which surprises them both. Tim is overjoyed and, with a nod from Sarah, we run from the house, through their garden and onto the castle lawns. The lime trees seem sad, dripping with water and weeping their bare branches right down to the lawn, which is littered with twigs and the remains of the snow.

Tim picks up a stick and throws it high in the air. I run and try to catch it, but it bounces in front of me, and I grasp it as it leaps up. Tim drops onto one knee, cuddles me and tries to say my name. It's a name he has shouted a thousand times, but now he can't seem to find it. We cuddle even harder, and I suddenly know why Sarah has been crying.

Tim returns to the cottage, and I hide below my cedar tree. Why is everyone I love hurting so much? What can I do?

My ears prick up at the sound of the gravel crunching. Andy has arrived in his old red car, and Harry in the one he hates to get dirty. We are clearly about to have our end of season sporting party with our friends, so why hasn't Nigel told me? He will have been planning this event for weeks, yet he expects me to be ready in a few minutes! What if I had planned to play with a young guest on the lawns, or to hunt rabbits with a visiting dog?

Andy and Harry move into the sitting room, and I join them as they talk and sip tea. They want to know how the season has gone, how the next few days will be - and, of course, they want to hear about the body!

Now, these are old friends, who have been coming here for years and know the valley well. Nigel has told them where I made my discovery and, straight away, they can picture it. They pat me and say what a clever boy I was. You may think it churlish of me, but I am annoyed. If they have nothing intelligent or helpful to say, I will leave them to their senseless chatter. I wander through to the hallway, and my sofa.

Sarah appears and looks at me, as one conspirator to another. I talk to people through their eyes. Yes, I can hear their words and know what they are saying, but their eyes often convey something different. I stand by her, so she can stroke me - I know she needs me. I also know Tim is ill, I saw that in his eyes. Soon Sarah will tell me herself, very soon, and let me know what I can do to help.

I hear the door open, and Nigel comes in. I always feel better when he's here. And who's that with him? Joe…and Kate! Kate is the same age as me and a very good-looking Spaniel! Now I know for sure it's time for friends - hurrah, my favourite time. The two of us shoot out of the castle and across the lawns, down to the lake. Kate's liver and white coat shines in the afternoon sun and, as she drinks the cool water, her high, glossy bottom is exaggerated by the vigorous wagging of her tail.

I race into the trees, through an area that grew thickly in the summer, but which is now flattened by frost and snow, and on to a big beech tree. Around the trunk, two or three holes have been opened, and paths lead from them to the lawn, where I have seen rabbits play and graze. Kate joins me, and we take it in turn to sniff each burrow, ending at the largest. Although she lives in a town and has far less practice than me, her instinct is good, and instinct is everything to a Spaniel.

'I think there are a couple of families here, don't you?', she says, looking to me for agreement. I'm too busy admiring her to respond.

Suddenly, she turns towards the castle. 'Joe's calling!', she shouts as she runs off. Is he? I heard nothing. Am I going deaf, I wonder, or am I in love? I smile to myself and follow her back to the castle. I want to ask her about the body. She travels more than me and knows more about the world; she will have the answer!

The morning breaks bright and clear, and I know that today we will have the best of sport. Nigel looks very serious, rushing around, trying to make everyone eat their breakfast, collect their kit and decide which vehicle they are going in - and all at the same time, which, it seems, should have been several minutes ago.

Kate and I have already toured the lawn. In fact, we could have done it twice by the time the party starts to emerge. The men are sometimes putting things in, or taking things out of vehicles, and sometimes just breathing the air, but always slowly. They suddenly realise we are not with them. Joe starts to whistle and Nigel to shout (because he can't whistle) and we leave our lair beneath my cedar tree and run to them. They both pretend to be angry, as if it's our fault they almost forgot us, but we have seen it all before and simply jump in the Land Rover.

Billy leads the way, and Kate and I are with Nigel and Joe in the last vehicle, in case anyone gets lost. I have told Kate what we are doing today - at least, what Bill, Billy's old Labrador, told me we are doing. And, as I gauge our route by the bumps and lurches of our journey, I know we will be starting just where he said.

We draw up in an old yard and Billy walks over to check everyone knows where to go. I glimpse Jasper, a small and very cheeky terrier, who is always part of the line. I know it's silly, but I can feel the excitement growing in me, and I sense it in Kate too. We have done this so many times, but still, I am excited.

Kate moves very close to me. 'So, it was in the area that floods most. The wet ground below the road and along from the big oak tree', she says, and fixes me with her big, brown eyes.

I forget I haven't filled her in with the details of my great adventure.

'Yes', I reply. 'Quite near the edge, where the rushes are thick, and you found the woodcock last year.'

She nods, and then continues. 'They think the body was washed down stream overnight, probably from the loch bridge, don't they?'

'Do they?', I reply. 'Who are "they"?'

'The police, the experts or whoever; at least, that's what Nigel says.'

I hate it when I'm not told. When things that concern me are left unsaid.

'Well, that's not right', I say. 'The body was there at least the day before, and maybe before that.'

Kate's eyes widen. 'How do you know?'

'Because I saw it there', I say quietly.

'Why didn't you tell someone?', Kate demands.

'Because no one asked me!', I protest.

Before Kate can say any more, Nigel opens the lunch barn door. I leave a bewildered Kate and disappear inside.

Freddie, Billy's assistant, is trying to save the fire. Billy always lights it first thing on a sporting day, and it usually goes well, with him energetically letting everyone know it is he who is to be thanked for the roaring blaze and warm room that welcomes them. Although it is Billy who lights the fire, it is Freddie who stokes it up when he comes back from the early morning feeding of the outlying woods. Now, whether Freddie forgot, or was delayed today, I don't get the chance to find out, but Billy's angry silence hangs heavily as Freddie works away.

I slide quietly under the table as Nigel pours coffee, passing the mugs to the team as they enter with comments that more wind is needed to test such expert sportsmen.

I remember the birds we dogs worked hard to find last year, how well they flew in the strong wind that blew all day, and how few were bagged!

I go outside to find Kate lying by Jock, Freddie's fat Labrador. Jock is already going grey around his eyes and is not looking forward to today. He is a good-natured dog and was, I've been told, fearless in his youth. But, as I look him in his eyes, I see they are becoming cloudy, and his fur has lost its shine.

'This will be your last season, old boy', I say to myself; 'I hope you enjoy it.'

The beaters, including Jasper, the terrier, have already left and I know Freddie and Jock would normally be with them. Perhaps they have a different job today. Before Jock can tell me, Billy strides up, calling Bill. He jumps into his Land Rover and roars off. In seconds the yard is quiet and empty; only the sound of a farmyard cockerel, cattle chewing loudly on hay and the distant murmuring of men drinking coffee breaks the peace.

Suddenly it comes back to me: the way I barked at Nigel to everyone's annoyance; his look, as he knew I needed him to follow me; the shock on his face as he saw the body and realised what was floating before him...

'So, what else are you hiding?', Kate says, keen to find out more.

I think about the body, and how the pheasant had been tightly clasped. I think of the times I have swum there, looking for a bird on the far bank, or one caught up in the shallows. I know the currents, the deep hollows, and the areas where rushes control the flow. There is no way a body could float downstream like that.

'Oh, this and that', I reply casually, and roll over to let Kate know I have said enough for now.

The sun comes out and we enjoy its warming rays until Nigel emerges with a worried look that says,

'We should have moved off five minutes ago - why didn't someone tell me?'.

The area is transformed from one of tranquillity to near panic. Kate and I snuggle down on the old sack and smile to each other. We know we have a glorious day ahead of us and that when the birds start to fly, all will be well.

Soon, I am the only dog at the back of a wood. A cock pheasant flies out and tries to go up the small valley behind me. Harry shoots, the bird must be down, and Nigel waves me away. I race to where I think he landed, and then search for his scent in the thick undergrowth. His scent weakens, have I lost him? I hunt to the side where an old thorn bush has blown over and become covered in ivy, but he isn't there, so I retrace my steps and make for the burn. His scent becomes strong again and I literally bump into him as I frighten him from his hiding spot. He is now at Nigel's feet, and I am panting with the joy that only comes after a successful retrieve.

The birds are flying the other way now and I have time to look across the valley. A car drives along the side of the wood and stops at the barn - Sarah has come to bring lunch. All this is part of the day, our day. It's a day with much talking and laughing and eating, when we dogs must wait and think how many more birds we would find if we were in charge!

Kate is desperate to hear more about the body and I am keen to tell her but enjoy making her wait.

She gives me a hard stare. 'What else should they know? Perhaps we can solve the mystery ourselves'.

This is just what I want to hear, and I fill her in about the pheasant, and how it was clasped firmly in the dead man's hand.

'We'll slip down there tomorrow', she says, her eyes wide. We can start to find out what really happened!'

When darkness falls, we return to the castle and continue the party. It's a special night, the men are dressed in what they call 'kilts', and the ladies are in fine dresses. Kate and I rest under the table.

We are woken by the noise of the main course being cleared. Joe is asleep but soon he will wake too and is likely to stretch out and kick one of us if we stay. We go into the hallway, walk quietly to the huge front door and wait for the party to move through to the bar, where they will be occupied for hours. I hear them pushing back their chairs and talking loudly, then the room breaks out into laughter - someone must have told a joke. Eventually, Harry comes through, gives Kate a pat and opens the door. We are away!

The moon is shining in a starry sky, which is not what I want at all! We can see clearly right across the lawn, which glows with frost, and two, no, three rabbits are there, just out from the trees. Our plan is to creep around behind them and cover their path as they run home; the trick is to make sure they don't see us first.

Quickly, I tell Kate to follow me, and we run the other way, behind the castle and the lake, always keeping off the lawn and out of the moonlight. Eventually we are at the beech tree and it's darker here. At first, I can't find the rabbits' track, but then I sense where they've run and follow it. We come out from behind a low bush and the lawn is in front of us and there they are, silhouetted by the moon.

We are about to rush them when Kate shows me another silhouette, approaching from the far side of the lawn and I can hardly believe my eyes. It's a large dog fox, the biggest I have seen for years, and we need to think quickly. Kate beckons me to the side, behind a low bush and we wait. The fox is clearly after our rabbits, and I understand what Kate has in mind. She believes they will want to run home - and we are perfectly placed to grab them! They must see him soon, he's so clear, yet his approach is so slow he seems almost motionless. As I watch his stealthy advance, the rabbits suddenly spy him and shoot off, straight for us.

There are two, side by side. I plan to take the far one, sure that Kate will take the near one. I wait, then lunge at my target, but, just as I picture my mouth closing around it, I am hit from the side and sent sprawling into a tree. As I get up, angrily, I see Kate is beside me, also angry at what has prevented her from taking her prize. We look at each other and laugh, we had both chosen the same rabbit and collided in the process. The lawn is still bathed in moonlight, but is now empty except for the fox, which looks at us from the far side before disappearing into the shadows.

The men are in the bar, showing clearly through the large windows. As I look at them, I hear them too, discussing the sport they enjoyed today and are looking forward to tomorrow. I am thinking of tomorrow too, and of showing Kate where I found my body.

3

In the morning, the valley opens out below us as we bounce our way from the castle. Our view changes as we lurch, turning from heather hill to lush grassland. When we stop for a moment, the woods take shape out of the morning mist and each one brings back its own memories, of soaring birds that got away and of others that nearly did, until I achieved another of my brilliant retrieves.

My eyes are drawn to the flood, which is lower now, and to the river above it. Could the body have floated to where I found it? I know I've asked myself this before, but I need to be sure. Even if he had been alive then, could he have held the bird in his grasp long enough and would he have ended up where I found him? No, the longer I look, the more certain I become. He couldn't have been carried by the water, so how did he get there?

Nigel's voice shakes me from my thoughts and soon I'm lost in my favourite world, where the bushes are thick, the grass tangled and the trees dripping with so much icy water I am totally soaked. The scent of birds running forwards is strong and I want to rush after them, but Nigel calls me back. At last, two pheasants spring up in front of me, swing to the side, and then turn and climb as they fly to where the guests are waiting. I watch eagerly. Will they fly on or coming crashing down and, if so, where?

Kate is the other side of the wood, and I know she is busy too. Several shots sound from there, rolling across the valley like thunder, and several birds flash over the trees from her direction. We go on through the day, doing bits of wood we haven't done before, or in a different way. Sometimes I am pushing through thick cover and then I'm standing behind Nigel, waiting. Sometimes I am with Kate, and sometimes I'm alone; but I'm always very wet! At the end, we hop into the Land Rover and curl up, the old sack steaming as we pant with exhaustion and happiness.

The failing light brings the end of the day; the barn door closes, the last man has gone in. We nose open the rear door of the truck – at last our other work can begin.

Although the light is fading, we know the spot well and anything we find will be through scent and memory, not sight. Everywhere has been flattened by the police. I try to tell myself it's nothing more than looking for a lost bird, but I feel faint when I picture the body. Kate walks a little upstream, and then out into the boggy area. She stands for a few minutes, looking about, but says nothing. I expect her to question me, to want to put what I have told her into reality, but she just turns away and heads towards the lunch barn, and the comfort of the old sack. She has clearly seen enough!

The next morning breaks bright and clear. Already, yesterday's sporting day is becoming a memory, though my aching legs remind me of it. Joe and Kate headed off at first light, but they will be back tomorrow, so I have little time to recover.

Andy leaves in the mid-afternoon, the last to go. Nigel bids him farewell and walks indoors, but I stay on the lawn. The sun breaks out and I lie down to enjoy it, over where we saw the fox. The lake is behind me, but I can hear the waterfall clearly and feel the cool of the chilled ground creeping through my fur, numbing the ache.

What will Kate have made of the spot where I found the body? Before I can find an answer, I hear footsteps approaching, crunching on the ice and the beech nuts. Two people and they stop just a few yards from the bush I have crept under. At last, they speak – it's Ian and Gwen.

They sound as Nigel and Billy do when they are planning a day and not agreeing. They obviously want to be secret, but what about? I want to hear what they say, but they are moving away, and the breeze is taking their words with it. They didn't see me, and now I know they have something to hide I will be ready; their secret will not evade me for long!

The friends' days have come and gone, but I can't rest. I try to tell myself it's because I'm too tired or too achy, but I know that's not true. Now that the buzz of the sporting days has died down, the pain of Tim comes pushing through and I'm drawn to him. I'm scared. He has become a Tim I don't know! I fight back the fear and make for the door, when suddenly it opens and Joe and Kate come in.

I stand there for a moment, torn between my need to be with Tim and a sense that Kate needs me too. Kate wins. She gestures towards the garden; we head out across the lawn and slide under the cedar tree. She is in a rare state. I have never seen her like this. She is breathing hard, and her eyes are as if she has seen a bird where there is no bird!

'What is it?', I ask.

She starts her story.

'We went to visit Joe's old friend, Paul. Joe had left me in the car, and I was soon asleep, but it was a restless sleep and produced a terrible dream.' I hear her heart pounding again, and she breathes in shorter and sharper gasps. 'I dreamt that Joe would die in an accident and that I would be injured. I also dreamt that Joe's friend Paul would have an accident and that his dog, Pip, would be thrown forwards and killed.

Later, after we got home, Joe received a phone call – my dream about Paul and Pip had come true! Pip is dead, Mutley; really dead! You know I have sensed things before: the number of birds we will bag, a guest who will be late…Remember when the old man fell over and broke his leg? I had said at the beginning of the day that someone would be injured. What if I am right again this time, how can we save Joe?'

I had hoped when she arrived that she would have an answer for me, a solution to my mysterious man who had become a body, but she just talks of more death. All I can see are questions, when what I need are answers!

It's early and Kate is still asleep. Nigel is away, so is Billy and, possibly, Joe too. Where have they gone? I don't know. All I do know is that they left very early this morning, and I have taken the chance to walk up to Billy' kennels to speak to the new dog.

There are four kennels in two pairs. They are built of stone and their outruns are topped with rusty railings. Bill lives in the right hand one, though his door is open, so he must have gone with the men. Everything seems unnaturally quiet, and I wonder if the new dog is away too, till his face appears nervously in his doorway.

He walks slowly to the tall gate. The railings shine where he has rubbed his nose and, as he reaches me, I see that his nose is sore and he carries his tail without wagging it. His head is small for a Labrador, and I sense a deep intelligence hiding behind the fear that fills his eyes. I want him to tell me who he is and if he knows the man I found floating that day? Yet, straight away, I know that terror haunts him.

'Shall I call you Ben'? I say, hoping he will correct me with his real name, but he just looks blankly into the sky. What could make a dog, who has clearly been well cared for, so full of fear? He must be involved with my body!

'I'll come again soon', I tell him. 'Perhaps we can have a walk together and talk some more?' He simply turns and walks back inside his kennel, his face full of sadness and confusion.

When I arrive back at the castle I see Gwen, and she is smiling! I haven't seen her smile for days. She wanders, full of life, from the cottage that she shares with Nigel and me, to the castle, humming some awful tune. I know why. She is hoping to see more of Nigel now the season is over.

Nigel is in the gunroom. He will have been cleaning and putting things away till he needs them for the new season, and he will be hiding! Eventually, he comes down, smiling sadly. He pats me. Gwen is in the hall, hovering, like a stoat waiting for a rabbit to appear from its burrow.

Has she changed since she came nearly a year ago? Maybe a little. Her eyes are the same dark blue, but they had less confidence back then. She had come to nurse Nigel's dying father, though her eyes were empty till Nigel appeared; after that they were always on him. She knew what she wanted, and old William saw it too. I was lying beside his bed when Nigel came in one day and Gwen had gone to fetch a pillow.

He held out his hand to Nigel and said, 'Be careful, son'.

Nigel hadn't been able to believe that she wanted him and now he doesn't know what to do. His eyes are those of a pheasant in a strange wood - they don't know where to fly! He is lost in a world he doesn't know, and, like the pheasant, his days of freedom seem numbered.

🐾

Joe and Kate have gone to see an old friend. I am at the lunch barn, where the clear up from the sporting season continues, with as much joy as if someone has died, but it has little to do with the body. In fact, now that the police have gone it is hardly mentioned.

Nigel tells me they think they know who the man was, the body that had been a man, but he doesn't say who. I don't think he knows himself, otherwise why wouldn't he tell me? The police seem to think it was an accident, so that must be that!

The sun is shining and casting crazy patterns on the wooden floor. Nigel and Sarah are making an unnecessary noise as they clear things away, and I am struggling to pick up the gossip from Bill. We are lying in the sun, just by the open door.

'How's the new dog', I ask.

'Oh, he just keeps himself to himself', Bill replies without emotion. 'Billy is fed up with him. He says if he doesn't settle soon, he'll get rid of him.'

'Have you spoken to him; found where he came from?', I ask, more with hope than expectation.

Bill shakes his head; 'I did at first, but he just turns away and won't answer, so why should I bother?'

I nod and think of mentioning Kate's dream but decide to keep my worries to myself and take a deep breath of morning air, perhaps it will clear my mind. The noise inside stops, and the dust starts to settle. I wander slowly indoors and find Nigel and Sarah in the kitchen. They are washing up but are talking much more than washing and Sarah has been crying again. They hear me approach and both turn, but when they see it's only me, they continue, and I lie under the table.

They are discussing Oliver. I wonder if Sarah cries for Oliver as much as for Tim, and whether Nigel cries for his little brother too. Sometimes, when Oliver comes to see Nigel, he talks to me. He is not a sportsman, and it's good to be treated as a friend.

I remember last year, just when the bluebells were going over in the middle wood, I went with Nigel to check on the cover crop there. Oliver was organising the sowing and, whilst Nigel and Billy talked, we talked. He said very little but, as you know, I listen to men's eyes more than their voices and Oliver's spoke of pain; pain and sadness!

This is not the sadness I feel when a bird flies the wrong way, or a day that I've looked forward to is cancelled. No, it is a deeper sadness that never goes away. Oliver isn't deaf and doesn't have a sore foot - in fact, he looks very healthy - but underneath I sense he is ill and that this adds to poor Sarah's pain.

※

Kate and Joe have gone, but Kate's face still haunts me. With the season over, we may not meet again for weeks, and all I can do is hope that when we do, she will be smiling, and her fears will be forgotten. I can't get the worry about Kate and Sarah, Tim or Oliver out of my head and lie awake wondering how it will work out and what I can do. I think of Gwen and her strange talk with Ian and, floating above them all is the body! I hoped Kate would have an answer for me, a solution to the mystery of the body, but her 'cloud' over Joe is all-consuming.

A little earlier, the police drove past the castle and on, through the farmyard towards the valley. I hoped Nigel would take me that way this morning, but he didn't. Jane tells me they were looking for a gun. Well, they can look as much as they like now that the season is over!

I retreat to my cedar tree. Again, a cold wind is driving rain across the lawn. It has come suddenly and takes my thoughts to the flood and its body. The chill and the spray appear from my memory and the man is as sharp as the day I found him.

Had I seen him before? I ask my memory for a face, one I could recognise, but nothing comes. I think of his body, of the pheasant clasped firmly, and know something is wrong, something is missing, but what? He hadn't floated down stream, I am sure, so had he just fallen?

Suddenly, I see it - or rather, what I didn't see. Where was his gun? Where was his bag? If he had floated in the floodwater, they wouldn't be by the body, but I know he didn't float, so they should be there! Where are they? Are the police thinking the same way or are they just tying up loose ends?

4

Sarah's voice lifts me from my daydream. She is speaking to Tim, who seems unhappy, so I take him for a walk on the lawns. Everything is so difficult for him now and he seems too sad to speak. I run ahead to where my camp is hidden below the roots of a scraggy old pine tree, barking with excitement. A rabbit leaps up in front of me and I race after it, determined to show Tim how fit I am, but it turns sharply and disappears down its hole. I expect Tim to laugh, to make fun of me, as the old Tim would have - but this Tim doesn't. I watch him as he turns and heads for home; no goodbye, no anything.

An hour later, I am still on the lawn. Everything is quiet today, too quiet. I am looking up into a tree, thinking about roosting pheasants, when I hear a voice. Tim is coming towards me, calling my name, as if he has just woken up. He runs past me and off towards the scraggy tree.

'How's your camp, Mutley? You were still digging it last year; it must be huge now.'

I follow him eagerly. I want to know why he can speak now when he couldn't before? Why our meeting this morning has gone from his mind? Was it ever there? But, for now, I'm just happy to have my old Tim back!

Tim and Sarah have driven off and I have wandered through into the castle sitting room. I listen to the crackle of the fire and, beyond, I hear the murmuring of cooks in the kitchen. My loyal team are working hard to do their jobs, leaving me to act as overseer. It is easy for the team, who each have their own duties, to miss something that I don't. This could be an old lady who is quietly waiting in the sitting room without anyone noticing, or a couple who want to take a walk but don't know where to go. I am there to look after them, so the team can get on with their work.

Everything checked, I leap onto my sofa and want to rest, but Gwen comes in and disturbs me. She seems ready for the kill. As you know, I'm bred to find game, and to do this I must understand it so, as Billy would say, I must think like a pheasant. It dawns on me that understanding Gwen is the same as understanding pheasants. With this realisation comes a thought that makes me smile. Suddenly the problem is one I understand and one I am sure I can solve, with a little help!

'The body has been identified', Nigel shouts, as he puts the phone down and turns to Jane and Ian. He says a name, but it means nothing to me. As I told you, they worked out who it must be last week, but now someone who actually knew him has seen the body. What may be important, though, is that he was a guest here five days before he was found. I think back to when I first saw the body. It was the day after New Year's Day, so I try to remember when we went out before that - when did we host a party?

It was snowing, yes, that must have been the day, and everyone was wrapped up. The birds didn't want to fly, but no one could have seen them even if they did, and at the end of the day the guests went straight home. I try to remember the body; did I look at the face? No, I've told myself this before! Why is the face so important? I don't know. I want to ask Nigel if they still think he floated there, right to where I found him, but he has gone.

I see I'm not needed and wander outside to enjoy the sunshine. The old pine near my underground camp protects it from the wind, and a clump of snowdrops is pushing through. They will soon be joined by the aconites and crocus. In the lake, the frogs and toads will soon be moving, emerging from the rotting leaves to mate and enjoy the sunshine. Archie, a terrier, once told me that toads were very tasty, and I believed him, but I soon spat it out and didn't try one again!

Yes, spring is here today. The lawn is drying, and I can really run across it, but my mind feels torn between Tim, Kate and the body. Tim, I will see shortly; Kate, I can only dream of seeing, and the body is a dream I don't want to see, but which won't go away! I'm sure Kate will know how to solve my problems, but I can't see her without Joe and, now that the season is over, he may not be here for weeks. I lie down and try to think of a way of causing a visit, but when I open my eyes, it's getting dark. I have slept for most of the afternoon, am none the wiser and am rather stiff.

In the morning, I'm by the summer house. It's an old wooden building that's recently been repaired and the smell of fresh paint still fills the air, and my nose! I have been drawn here by what Kate would call a 'cloud'. She has become an expert on them, though how much she truly 'sees' and how much is down to her clever thinking, I don't know. She is certainly concerned about Joe and has sensed a danger. Do I sense danger in what has drawn me here? As someone who is new to this 'cloud' idea, I don't know, but I am certainly uneasy.

The concrete floor is chilling my feet and whatever has drawn me here must show itself soon. I move beside the old holly bush that fills most of the gap between the summer house and the lake. I am about to take a drink but hear voices and roll on my side beneath the overhanging branch. It is Ian and Gwen.

'Is he eating out of your hand yet?', Ian begins, and sits on one of the new bench seats. Gwen follows him. From my hideout I can only see a small part of the sun-bathed room, but suddenly Gwen's shadow appears over Ian. Her hand comes into view and flicks through his hair. I hear her sit next to him as he carries on.

'So, what's your next move? Have you done enough to be certain he will propose, or will he need pushing?'

Ian's voice carries a menace that makes me wriggle and I'm afraid he'll hear me, but he continues.

'Give him a day or two and, between us, your man will be as good as signed up within the week.'

I can't see them now, they have moved below my sight line, but I can sense how close they are. I want to move, to race to wherever Nigel is and warn him, but I also know there is more I need to know. I must remember that Gwen has been weaving her magic for a while now and Nigel will need a lot of convincing.

Eventually they leave, Gwen heading in the direction of her cottage and Ian directly back to his desk in the castle. When I'm sure they've gone, I move from my lair and nearly fall over with stiffness.

I walk towards the cottage, confused, trying to focus - and suddenly Gwen is there, standing below the chestnut tree. Her car door is open, and she's leaning inside. The tree is casting shadows, but there can be no mistake. Gwen is removing something, something that looks very like a shotgun!

But she doesn't shoot, and the season is over. What would she be doing with a gun? I need Kate and her cloud busting more than ever!

I am woken by the ringing of Nigel's phone. It is early, very early, and he hasn't even been down to make tea. He came back last night – I heard the creaking of the stairs as he went up – and I wonder if I know enough yet to convince him that Gwen is a fraud.

I hear him speaking to Gwen and sense the phone call was bad news. He must have woken her, and he never does that! The sound of low voices filters down the stairs and I creep up to hear better. It hits me as if I had been struck by one of the delivery lorries that thunder down the castle drive. Joe is dead!

My thoughts immediately go to Kate. How is she, has she been injured too, as she foresaw? I muscle unnoticed into the bedroom and lie at the foot of the bed. Yes, I hear Nigel say, they think it was an accident, somewhere late last night.

Why don't they mention Kate? Please mention Kate…and then they do! She must come and stay, they agree. I can't contain myself and rush around to Nigel's side of the bed.

'It's okay old boy', he says, rubbing my nose. 'We'll look after her, won't we?'

But he's crying, and I know it's not okay; he has lost one of his best friends.

Morning comes before sleep, and I walk onto the lawn. Today, everything important is happening in the marquee, so that's where I am. It has been decided to replace the wooden floor and bar, and Peter and his team have started work on levelling the base before fixing the new timber. Ian and Gwen are nowhere to be seen, though I heard their voices earlier and it made me shiver again.

The talk in the marquee reminds me of Billy on a bad day and, as you know, I have learnt to stay clear of men on days like this. Nigel is not here. He left early this morning and, although I was by his side as he drove off, I don't think he noticed me. Is he going to fetch Kate?

I wander out to the ancient fir tree that looks down over the marquee and lie beneath its branches. The view is not as good as from the cedar tree, but this is where my old friend Gunner is buried. He was a sheep dog here and I feel I need his strength. I wonder if Kate has been hurt. She was right about Joe's death and I'm afraid she will have been right about her own injury too.

The sound of sawing and nailing drifts over from the marquee, and a car draws up in Sarah's drive. Jane comes outside, calling my name and shading her eyes from the sun. I lift myself from my sadness and go to her with as much enthusiasm as I can muster. She has a plate of my favourite food, a juicy piece of steak left by a lunch guest. She watches me eat it, though it sticks in my throat, and I think I'm going to choke. Eventually, I swallow. She strokes me and, reassured, heads back inside.

I settle in a sunny spot beside the waterfall. Here I can relax and see Nigel when he returns. I watch Oliver driving his pickup along the farm track and believe Tim must be home too. The hours pass, darkness falls, and still there is no sign of Nigel.

During the night I lie awake, hoping to see Nigel - and Kate – but I am exhausted, and sleep takes over.

Suddenly, I wake and the first thing I see is Nigel's coat, thrown carelessly over a kitchen chair. I leap to my feet and sniff. The smell of Nigel is fresh but, try as I might, I can't smell Kate. Part of me wants to race upstairs, to wake Nigel and demand to know what is happening. But another part, the one that wins, is afraid of what he will say. I dread the news that Nigel might have brought home but tell myself to go back to sleep. It is very early and today will be difficult enough.

5

So many thoughts are racing around in my head, and I try to concentrate on the happy ones, which I'm glad to find come easily. I remember the time when Kate and I had just met, both young dogs and very nervous in our first season with the older dogs. I am immediately struck by her beauty. We are in the line below a steep bank and Nigel and Joe are next to each other. I hear the birds take off with a determined cry and know they are above us; men shout and guns fire, but my eyes are fixed on Kate, and I know she will always be important to me.

My daydream is broken by the creaking of the landing floor, it must be Nigel. I race up the stairs and meet him at the top. Kate is alive, he tells me, but she is very shaken, and her shoulder has been injured.

'I took her to the vet yesterday, and we know it isn't broken, so some good rest and sympathy should see her right.'

He emphasises the word 'rest' and I take this to mean no racing after rabbits. I am about to ask when she'll be with us when he continues.

'I'm collecting her today. We leave in half an hour; will you be ready?'

That was yesterday - and what a day! Although I am now wide awake, I slept very little and only woke a few minutes ago. I look across the kitchen, from my bed to Kate's, and see it fitting neatly beside the Aga, where she is sleeping the deepest sleep.

It was around lunchtime yesterday when we arrived at Kate's vet, where a tall, slim, man met us. Just the man for striding up rough ground after grouse, I thought, as he showed us through to the kennels at the back. Kate was very pleased to see us, and the sound of her tail wagging on the bars of her pen was like the church bells ringing on a Sunday morning. She wanted to hop down and run to me, but the vet stopped her. Nigel bent down and picked her up, cradling her in his arms.

She lay on the back seat of the car as we travelled home, with me beside her. After a while, she opened her eyes and I could see she wanted to speak but didn't know where to start, so I began.

'Did you always go with Joe when he was out in the evening?'

Kate smiled a pained reply.

'No, of course not, but we had been out all day, and on the way back he had called on an old friend of his for supper.'

The thought that she would never be with Joe again made her stop. She looked tired, and I was going to let her sleep, but then she opened her eyes and continued.

'I had been sleeping in the car while the men ate in the house. I remember Joe getting into the car and starting the engine. I had been on the back seat but moved to the floor because I remembered there were several bends near the house that he always took quite fast, and I didn't want to be thrown about. Anyway, on the second bend, or it may have been the third, something made me look up. A car was coming at us on the wrong side of the road. We swerved to miss him and hit a tree. The rest you know'.

She turned and looked out of the window, and I knew she had said all she wanted to.

No, I thought, I don't know! Well, I knew Joe was dead, but what I wanted to know was whether she had felt any more dreams; more 'clouds'? Did she see the accident before it happened? All of this is fresh in my mind; I must ask her as soon as she's ready.

Now I am on the lawn, leaving Kate to rest in the kitchen, and I am frustrated. I know I shouldn't be, and that after the accident it will take her a while to regain her strength. Yet, I have always pictured her as a super fit dog who could overcome anything. Is her fitness the problem, or does she have other worries? The loss of Joe must have hit her hard -

and that she saw the accident coming and couldn't stop it must make it worse!

I wander over to the rabbit burrows, the ones Kate and I examined before our friends' sporting day. I remember our attempts to ambush the rabbits and the dog fox who stood so proudly. I take a deep sigh as I realise the following day was Joe's last.

I want action, something to occupy my mind and lift Kate from a past she can do nothing about. We have few visitors and only the occasional wedding interrupts the team from its spring cleaning. The lawn is large and with the next wedding close I must check all is well.

The area in front of the castle is open, open enough for me to have a good run. I have come to a halt and am breathing hard when something catches my eye by the castle door. It's Kate. I don't think she should be out - in fact, I'm sure she shouldn't - but fresh air must do her good, mustn't it? No harm can come of it, as long as we don't run.

'I want to hunt rabbits,' she says. I look at her bandaged leg, and smile.

'Okay, Mutley, I'll walk very slowly and make the rabbits run, and you show me just how fit you are!'

We start by the lake, moving around towards the gate and then the drive that runs down from it. I want there to be many rabbits, but today there are none. We see several in the field beyond Tim's house, and where they have eaten the grass and left their droppings, but there isn't one for me to chase!

As the sun warms up, we find a sheltered spot and rest. Nigel will soon notice that Kate is not in the cottage and come searching, but until then we will enjoy our own space and time.

A few hours later, we are back at the cottage, and I am looking at Kate. She has been asleep for much of the time since our walk to the lawn and has settled well into her new bed beside the Aga. She stirs and lifts her head.

'I couldn't remember it', she says, looking straight at me. 'But now it's coming back. The car came directly at us. I saw the driver's face for a second - no, not his face, his eyes. He meant it, Mutley, it was no accident. He meant to kill us.'

I am shocked. From anyone else I might doubt this, put it down to excitement or something, but not with Kate.

'They found me in the back of the car, with a bash on my head and shoulder, but Joe was lying beside it with scratches on his hands and a hole in his head. How do you explain that? Tell me, how?'

I have no answer. Exhausted, Kate closes her eyes, and sleep takes over once again.

I leave Kate sleeping and tour the castle. The marquee is restored, the new floor has been waxed and polished, and it now shines with a gentle glow. I want to be impressed but am still too dazed by what Kate has told me. I hoped she would join me, to continue what I'm sure she has only started to explain. The fire is roaring in the sitting room, and I wander over to sit by it, to take stock in the surroundings I know. But as I approach it, instead of warmth, a terrible shiver runs down me, and I know it's Kate.

I rush back to the cottage and find that, despite the warmth of the Aga, she's shaking too.

'Something terrible is going to happen, I don't know why, or when or to whom, I just know it is!' She looks at me with terror in her eyes and then rolls herself into a ball.

'Is it Nigel'? I ask, denying her clear desire to be left alone. 'I have seen Ian and Gwen plotting something against him. They are together – they are a couple and have been hiding it!'

I don't think Kate hears me, so although I feel better for saying it, again I must wait. I am shocked by this new 'cloud', for that's what it must be, and soon I must demand answers from her.

Two days pass, and finally she joins me. We are enjoying the sun by the front door of the castle. The thick hedge that leads to Tim's house is casting shadows to my left and, straight ahead, the old park and its rabbits look inviting. Kate is lying beside me. She can see the rabbits too and the 'cloud' she saw seems to have been pushed to the back of her mind.

'If you were half a dog, you would have caught them', she teases, looking at two rabbits that are staring out from behind a tree. I am amazed by her courage. How can she be so relaxed with so much weighing on her? I try to respond. I think of saying that even if she were fit, she wouldn't have caught them either - then realise that she probably would have, and just grunt a reply.

'What did you say about Ian and Gwen?', she says, without lifting her eyes from the rabbits.

I tell her how I saw them, of the tone in their voices and the shock it gave me.

'I'm not surprised, I saw them together last year. Joe and I disturbed them after one of your days up the valley. But you think it's more than a romance? Remember, you live a very sheltered life here.' She is now looking at me, wanting to see as well as hear my reaction.

I am stunned. She seems to take the deceit as acceptable! Then my senses regain their balance and I reply, 'Yes, I do. If they were merely being romantic, they wouldn't need to plot, to whisper as they did. They're hiding something, I know it.'

'But what?' Kate asks. I don't have an answer for her and simply shrug my shoulders.

'So, if Joe's death wasn't an accident, someone must have caused it, but who and why?' I ask, hoping my directness will impress her.

'I don't know, but it gives us two suspicious deaths, doesn't it? Deaths that may be linked – and that no one else seems to care about!'

A loud and painful sound breaks the air, interrupting us. It comes from the road, and then an ambulance with flashing blue lights races down Tim's drive. I see Nigel, Sarah and Oliver in the garden, then everyone rushes into the house. We are on our feet now and have moved to the hedge. Our view is poor, and we look at each other - what can it be? The last time I saw an ambulance rushing like this was when a guest collapsed. Has someone collapsed?

At last, they come out; Nigel first to check all is clear, and then the men with a stretcher, walking slowly. Memories of the stricken guest come rushing back, but worse. It must be Tim, as he is the only person not standing there. I want to race through and find out, but Kate stops me. Slowly the ambulance drives away, leaving Nigel and Oliver watching. Kate turns to me, her look of terror returning.

Morning arrives, and everything is unduly quiet. No one has moved in Tim's house and I'm not even sure if anyone is there. Here, in the castle, the preparations for the wedding go on in silence. Nigel is off doing Oliver's work, checking the animals and whatever else he does. I ask Jane what has happened, but she just strokes me. Kate is back in the cottage; the ambulance has upset her. It has brought back too many memories, and the new 'cloud' has left her confused. I push through the partly-open door and look at her. She stands, tries to stretch, and walks slowly outside. I close my eyes for a while, then suddenly Kate rushes in again, barking,

'They're back!'

Tim is very ill. He collapsed in his house and now he's in hospital. I ask Nigel what's wrong and he says they don't know. I'm not sure if this is right or if he just doesn't want to tell me. I search his eyes but see only pain and confusion. Kate stays in her bed. I could easily have stayed in bed too, but a wedding party is arriving tomorrow, and someone must make ready! Nigel is now in the farmyard; I can see his Land Rover across the valley, standing out clearly in front of the hay barn. Sarah and Oliver are visiting Tim, and I want to be there too. I want to be with all of them.

I nose my way into the castle. At first all seems very quiet, then I hear voices. Perhaps I should say I feel rather than hear them, because the first I know of them is a shiver. It starts behind my ears and then tingles down my back! The sound is coming from the office, the one behind the reception desk that is full of paper and electronic wires. I lie quietly by the door.

'It needn't affect anything; we must push on with our plans,' Ian says.

'Don't be silly, his best friend has been killed and now Tim is dying, he's hardly going to feel like proposing, is he?' Gwen replies, with more annoyance than grief. I rub an ear with a paw - am I hearing right? How can they think these things, let alone say them?

The bride arrives, noisily pushing open the castle door, and Ian comes running, false smile restored. She is carrying her wedding dress, and others follow with a huge array of baggage. They are joined by a large woman who seems to be called 'mother'.

My responsibility at weddings is entertaining children, but there are none today, so I just look and listen. I move unnoticed from behind the office door, still unable to believe what I have heard. Jane is on duty and flows effortlessly into a smooth, reassuring voice, all-encompassing smile and we-can-solve-any-problem manner. I am most impressed.

I have learnt that women are the prime people at a wedding, but I had taken this to mean the bride. Now I realise that big women called 'mother' are also important, I must remember it. I lie, shaking, on my sofa, whilst Ian and Gwen are once again playing the parts of loyal members of staff.

I am lying by the door, in case any more guests arrive, and am listening to their conversation, whilst trying to look asleep. Jane is telling 'mother' the times and places, and who should go where and when. Peter, the handyman, walks past me, carrying the bags to their rooms. I am angry; angry and confused by what I've just heard.

So, Ian and Gwen are working together, and they want Gwen and Nigel to marry; but why? This simple question bounces about in my head, waiting for an answer or, to be honest, for Kate to give me an answer. For all her 'clouds', that seems like it could be a long way off. Perhaps I should solve this mystery myself.

Did Ian and Gwen come at the same time? No, Gwen came before Ian, but only by a few months. I can remember him arriving last season, so it was winter, and Gwen came the previous summer, when Nigel's father's health became poor and he needed a nurse. Kate was here too. She will remember, I tell myself, as though my own memory can't be trusted. Everything seems to revert to Kate.

I force myself to think about the wedding. The nearest thing is a sporting day, and I understand that, but a wedding seems such a lot of work with not even a good bag of game to show for it! I take a deep breath and continue my wait by the door.

6

The problem with an early season wedding is the weather. Here, in the middle of Scotland, we are very unlikely to enjoy a hot, balmy day in early March. Even a calm and gently warm one seems impossible, and this makes my job as lawn manager very difficult. It's easy for the rest of the team to assume it will be wet, or cold, or both, and charm the guests with roaring fires and romantic candles. I can only make myself ready for the good weather when it does come. So, to build up my energy, I settle onto my sofa and wriggle myself comfortable. The sound of 'mother's' voice is merging with the sound of glasses and laughter from the bar.

It's Saturday, the wedding day, and a car arrives with a boy and girl keen to escape. While the parents smile and welcome old friends, we run out and play. It has been so long since I've had the chance for such games, I'd almost forgotten how much fun it is - and how unfit I have become!

The boy suddenly appears from among the branches of the same tree that Tim did just a few weeks ago, and I stop in my tracks. My mind is suddenly full of Tim and tears well in my eyes. The children think I've hurt myself, but then a parent calls and it's time for the little ones to get dressed for the wedding. From shrieking laughter to exhausted silence takes seconds, and all I can hear is my own heavy breathing and the singing of the birds.

From our cottage behind the castle, the one Kate and I share with Nigel and Gwen, I look out into the stable courtyard, watching as the smart wedding guests emerge from their rooms looking so different to the relaxed people I saw earlier. I want to run to them and make them relax again but I know I mustn't. I think of my friends - the illness of Tim, the sadness of Sarah, the pain of Oliver, the strangeness of Ian, the greed of Gwen - and all depending on poor Nigel, whom, I sometimes think, has only me looking out for him.

I hear a sigh; I have momentarily forgotten Kate. She has woken from her slumbers, slumbers that have taken up most of her time since Joe's death and the ambulance. She stands up and stretches carefully. Our vet removed her leg bandage yesterday and she now looks fully fit, though I know she's not. She noticed the guests arrive and I offered to show her what I do at weddings, but she shook her head and looked away. She is very down, and I have decided to let her rest. I hope the Kate I knew returns soon!

Evening has arrived and Sarah is home, though she hasn't been to the castle. Oliver must be back too because Nigel has stopped rushing off in the mornings. I see lights on in their house through the hedge and wonder if I should visit them.

A light goes out, the front door opens, and Sarah appears. She stands in her porch and looks up into the sky. When she sees me, a smile forms, stretches wide, and bright white teeth show in the moonlight. I run to her, and she bends down and cuddles me, holding me so tight I think one of us will choke, then she lets go and just looks at me.

'He's coming home soon, Mutley, and when he does, he'll need you more than ever. I know I've told you before, but he will, he'll really need you!'

In the morning, I look out and see the guests have gone. Ian is moaning and snow has begun to fall, so I settle where I am. The snow adds to the strangeness that has taken over my life. Just a short while ago everything was normal and predictable. One sporting day led into another. Everyone who should be there, was there, and they were fit and well. I look out on a sea of snow that is drifting across the drive and shiver, I need some me time!

Now, I hope you don't think I'm one of those soft dogs who moans when it's wet or cold, or likes to walk around with one of those awful tartan waistcoats that some dogs are willing to be seen in. There are times when I'm very happy to jump in a flooded river or exhaust myself in thick undergrowth that's covered in melting snow, but it needs to be in a good cause!

Let me tell you the tale of the big cock pheasant in the middle of winter. I hope, by using the word tale, you don't think the episode is untrue, or an exaggeration, because I assure you it all happened, just as I tell it. It was after Christmas, and we were down by the banks of our river, just before it flows under the road and then on towards the sea. I believe the river is well known for its salmon fishing, but to me it is important for the thickness of the undergrowth and the strength of the birds.

Here, old woodland follows the steep valley sides that fall to the small river below. I say small, because generally the water that flows between the large rocks and around the sharp bends is just a trickle, but after a day of heavy rain the flow becomes a torrent. Huge cascades of water throw plumes of white spray or create great whirlpools as they pass the large rocks. I heard the Labradors amongst us told not to enter the river and I totally agreed. Although some are keen, few are strong swimmers, unlike Spaniels.

The birds started to fly, a few shots were fired and then, suddenly, a bird appeared over an oak tree beside me and fell into the middle of the river. I didn't hesitate and leapt into the boiling water. It was a strange sensation. The water, although warmer than I expected, pulled me in all directions. I had the bird firmly in my sights and was about grab him when he disappeared, and everything became dark and quiet.

I discovered later that we had both been washed over a waterfall and caught up in the whirlpool below. The bird, being smaller, had soon been pushed out and started to float away, but I was caught there for several seconds (although it seemed like hours) before I, too, was pushed to the surface. Needless to say; my mind was still fully focused on the pheasant and as soon as I saw him, I was on him and back to the bank, the bird firmly gripped in my mouth. Several of the men told Nigel off for letting me enter the water, but I knew what I was doing.

These are some of the moments that stay in my memory and return as dreams by the fireside on cold nights. I am sure that sometimes, when I'm sleeping soundly on my sofa and give a quiet 'woof', that this will be one of the dreams.

Everything is silent. The blanket of snow is six inches deep and kills all sound. I force my way across the drive till I come to the tracks left by a vehicle. I follow them towards the road, looking around for any signs of rabbits, but the snow is as unmarked as the moment it dropped from the leaden sky. Where are the rabbits? They must still be hiding in their burrows.

When I reach the top of the garden, I hop out of the well-rolled track and spring my way to an area where the snow has been flattened and mixed with a mass of feathers. Something has eaten a pigeon here, could it have been a fox? I scent around and look for tracks but decide it must have been a hawk of some kind, and head back towards home.

Kate would enjoy this, yes, it would do her so much good, I decide, and hurry on. The snow reaches my belly and hangs there as small frozen balls. Tim's house is in darkness. I hope Sarah arrived at the hospital before the snow. Their drive has filled, and the snow reaches halfway up the box hedge and well up their front door.

I return to the castle and thaw out by the fire. The snow that had stuck to me melts and leaves wet patches on the carpet which, I am glad to say, everyone is too busy to notice. The warmth helps me sort my thoughts and I know I must concentrate on the two deaths; so much depends on it.

Once I have warmed up a little, I return to the cottage, where I find Kate looking out of the window. She joins me on the step where the cool of the snow chills the air. We stand and watch as a sheet of snow slides from the old stable roof and half blocks the path below. Kate laughs. One look and I know she wants to run, up to the lake, lap up some cool, refreshing snow and revel in the hope that a rabbit might be caught. As it is, we make do with a slow walk to the castle along a well cleared path and enjoy the heat of the fire there.

Kate looks at me and takes a deep breath. 'You want to know if I knew it would happen, don't you; if I foresaw Joe's crash?'

I nod a reply and wait.

'Yes, I think I did, at least in part, and any doubts I had were destroyed when I foresaw Tim's collapse. When we set off that evening, I had been sleeping on the back seat, a deep and strange sleep. Something told me to lie on the floor and, do you know, I have never lain there before. I know I said it was because the road had sharp bends, which it does, but I have been on that road many times and have never thought of moving onto the floor before. So, why then, why should I tell myself to lie where I have never lain and why did I suddenly look up as the other car hit us and the driver looked me in the eye, which undoubtedly saved my life?' She stops for breath, then continues,

'And those eyes, the eyes of the driver, I know them!'

'Who?', I demand. But she just looks incredibly sad and shrugs her shoulders,

'But I do know them!'

I need to restore her confidence, to lift her.

'And Tim?' I add, determined to know the answer.

Kate looks at the fire, as if too much is being asked of her.

'When I saw the 'cloud', I didn't know what it meant. It was like the one I had with Joe, but because I wasn't with Tim at the time, it wasn't clear who it was for. Now I'm sure it was for Tim.'

'And now you know it was for him, will he get better?', I ask.

Kate looks straight at me.

'I don't know, in some ways the cloud is still there, as it was before Joe's death. It may still have something to tell me', she says.

'So, it might not be about Tim!' I yap, as she makes to leave. 'It might be about Nigel, or Ian or Gwen; or the body, or anyone!'

Kate leads the way across to the cottage but doesn't answer. She walks slowly and with a slight limp. I know she believes Joe's death was not an accident. I must be patient and trust that she will see what happened, and then we can move on.

And the body, she still hasn't told me of her thoughts on him. I know she has them, thoughts and ideas, but somehow they must wait till her 'cloud' lets them through. Does her 'cloud' hold the answer to everything?

It's mid-morning and I'm lying on my sofa in the reception hall. Gwen has taken Kate to our vet for her final check-up. I offered to go too (though I hate vets), to give her support, but she said no.

Nigel appears, wearing his shooting breeks; short, baggy trousers with bright red tassels showing where his long woollen socks meet the tweed just below his knees. He hasn't worn these since the end of the sporting season, so why is he wearing them now?

He goes into his office, just behind the reception desk, but soon comes out when a tall man arrives with a golden Cocker Spaniel and small, blonde wife. They get into Nigel's Land Rover, and I follow them, introducing myself to the dog, whose name, it turns out, is Trudy. Soon we are bouncing up the track, the farm buildings and castle well behind us and Boundary Hill growing in front. I don't think it is the boundary of anything, but it is certainly the highest point for miles around. In places the snow has drifted right across the road, and I wonder if we'll make it.

Trudy is worried and lets out a whimper as we hit a bump that's hidden by snow. She is thrown sideways for a moment. I must admit, I am a little worried too, but this is no time to show fear and I lean into her, reassuringly. Nigel comes here when he's showing off the estate. He can point out all the woods, and where the valleys twist away and, as we are so high, can show how testing the sport will be.

Today the vista is a mix of whites, the loch and woods in contrast below us, caught in a flash of sunshine. The sight of it brings back old Gunner, the sheep dog. He fills my memory, forever swimming strongly. My eyes catch the river, and I shiver. It doesn't mean the same as it did before I found the body there. I know I must return, and soon. I must solve the mystery and return it to the happy place it used to be.

Here and there, the vivid greens of the fir trees stand out in the white landscape and Paul turns in his seat to point across the valley; he is impressed! We shake our way back to the castle. I sit on the old sack with Trudy, while the men jump down and chat. Trudy finally smiles, a smile I am confident I will see again!

As I trot back into the castle, having seen off our guests, I spy Kate lying on the sofa. All was well at the vet - I was sure it would be.

Nigel comes down from the gun room, taking the stairs several at a time and carrying an old cap. He tosses it to Kate, who opens her mouth and catches it with an energetic jump.

'This has arrived with some of Joe's things. It's too worn to wear; I thought you might like it.'

I watch him go. His smile tells of a successful show-round, and a good booking to come. I look at Kate. She has tucked the cap under herself, as a hen on eggs; it is bringing back too many memories. She hops down from the sofa and walks outside. I make to join her but am halted by the cap. It beckons me, so I hop up beside it, something nagging me. I hold it in my mouth, remembering Joe's scent and feeling the tears swell in my eyes.

I saw this pattern of tweed so often - Joe's whole suit was made in it. Breeks, waistcoat and jacket, all trying to flood me in memories. I remember him walking up a hill. The sun is shining but the wind is cold. It is catching his jacket, which he has undone, and blowing it out, showing his waistcoat. His face is red, almost purple, with the effort and he is breathing hard. Yet he has a broad smile, which tells of kindness. I will always remember his face.

Suddenly it comes to me. The feeling that has been with me since I first saw this cap has nothing to do with Joe but is to do with the pattern of tweed. The body wore this tweed, this very same pattern of tweed, Joe's tweed!

Peter walks hurriedly passed me, carrying boxes. I am amazed, he never hurries anywhere! I follow him. The marquee has been cleared and now stands empty and very big. I walk across the floor, careful not to leave tell-tale paw prints, and stop by the large French window. Nigel and Sarah are walking by the lake, laughing and smiling. They haven't seen me; I don't think they can see anyone. For a few moments, their troubles are forgotten.

Kate joins me, and we walk outside. Just last night a warm breeze replaced the chill, the snow has nearly gone, and everywhere is a mixture of sodden hollows and lonely patches of white where the warmth hasn't reached. The earth looks bland and lifeless.

I pick my way around the big puddles, but Kate runs straight through them, splashing loudly. So, she is now officially fit and seems determined to make the most of it. She runs ahead of me up to where we saw the fox just a few weeks ago and lies down. I lie beside her and turn to face her. She looks away, but I have waited long enough; questions must be asked!

'Do you remember when Ian first came here?'

She didn't expect the question, but she looks at me and smiles.

'Yes, I do; it must be last year, and he had been here less than a week when we came for the annual autumn day.'

I am amazed that she remembers it so clearly and, by the way she is looking at me, so is she! I am about to ask her more, when she continues,

'I remember it because Joe knew him and was surprised to see him here.'

Again, I am amazed. 'How did Joe know him? Was it a good reunion?'

Kate smiles.

'No, I don't think so. Few words were used, but their eyes spoke of mystery and surprise. Joe looked shocked and Ian very worried.'

I stand and look at Kate as seriously as I can.

'How did Joe know him'?

She just shrugs her shoulders.

'It must have been before my time.'

A thought comes to me, one that seems too simple, but that cannot be ignored.

'Think, Kate, were the eyes that looked so worried at that meeting the same eyes you saw in the driver at Joe's fatal crash.'

She thinks for a moment, knowing the significance of this, but then shakes her head.

'No, Mutley.'

So, now there is the new question of how Joe and Ian knew each other and, with Joe gone, we may never know. Did this meeting lead to Joe's death? Kate is certainly more positive, perhaps she'll remember more; her gifts seem to be increasing. Earlier she had asked why Nigel was dressed for a sporting day – but that was before either of us had seen him! At the time, I wondered what she meant, but when I saw him, I knew; her ability to 'see things' is growing.

7

The ground is cold. The snow has only just gone, but the sun is shining, and its warmth is finding its way into my back. I scratch my shoulder, a part I can never seem to reach. My summer coat must be coming through.

Today is the annual wedding fayre. A long van draws up and an old man with several assistants unload armfuls of dresses, which they carry into the castle. Before they have finished another van parks alongside, and flower-stands and boxes of leaflets are removed.

Soon the drive is full of coming and going, cakes, flowers, tall boards that hardly go through the doorway and bags of things too small for me to see from here. I leave my comfy spot below the cedar tree and follow a man carrying two hats, through the front door, past the desk and bar door, and on to the marquee itself. It is very busy, but there is nothing to eat yet, so I return to the lawn.

Guests start to arrive and I circulate, playing my part. I am used to these fayres now; I have helped with many. Steve, the chef, brings out food at various times during the day and I know I need to be here. Hillary (the girl with puffy cheeks) and her man Phil are by the hat stand, and I lead them to the food table in the middle of the marquee. A plate of fillet steak has just been put there – I'm already looking forward to a few tasty morsels tomorrow!

I have only seen Kate a couple of times this morning, and then from a distance. I hope she is noticing all the work I do. She is now lying under Gunner's tree, and I wonder if she's bored, but then I spy fear in her eyes. I go over to her. She has curled into the ball I have seen too often, a silent ball. I nudge her with a foot, a 'snap out of it' nudge, but she curls even tighter. She wants to be alone, so I let her be.

It's cooler now, and the rush of people that filled the marquee and spilled onto the lawn is just a few groups. I see the girls putting away their fine dresses and have just passed the man carrying his hats. I look for the girl with the cakes, or the remains of the food tasting, but the tables are bare. I will have to stay hungry a little longer!

Kate has returned to her bed by the Aga, and when Nigel brings a steak left from the wedding fayre, she just licks it and nibbles the edge, as old dogs do before they die. Should I moan at her till she moves? My instinct is to paw at her, to growl - she must know how much we all need her, how much we love her! But I sense she needs more time, so I leave her to rest and complete a tour of the castle. It has to be done, though I am in no mood for it. My checks reveal that everything seems to have been put straight after all the excitement.

A sound comes from Sarah's garden, a sound I know. Tim must be home! I smile as I eagerly push through the hedge and see Tim in his wheelchair. I want to ask him so much. When will he walk again and when can we play with a ball in the garden? But before he can answer Sarah pushes him indoors. I can see that her face wants to cry but she won't let it.

🐾

I have been resting after a rabbit hunt, when Kate springs from her bed as if one of those rabbits has just entered the room.

'Go to the office, Mutley, Nigel's office, go now, quickly!'

I have things on my mind, things I want to ask her, but see this is urgent so I move fast. Nigel has a pen in his hand and a sheet of paper covers the small desk. Gwen is hovering and Ian is in the corner. both of them looking at Nigel. I leap up, pressing a paw onto the table, my muzzle against Nigel's leg and bark with as much panic as I can muster. He has seen me like this before: when I found the body. I turn and run for the front door, hoping my act will be enough to make him follow. As I go, I hear tables moving and chairs falling, steps thundering after me. Perhaps they think it's another body?

I reach the door, but don't know what to do next. My actions have been spontaneous. I look at Nigel and, in that instant, I suddenly know what I must do. I look to the left, turn and run that way with him following. I sprint to the marquee entrance and then dive as far as I can down a big rabbit hole that has been dug near there. I lift my head, look at Nigel, and then dive again, barking frantically. Ian and Gwen catch up with us, as does Kate, who joins in the barking and starts scratching wildly at the hole.

'What is it?', demands Ian, with annoyance written clearly across his face?

'It must be a fox, probably looking for somewhere to have its cubs'. Nigel shouts, pretending to be excited too. He picks up a spade, starts to dig and continues,

'We can't have a litter so close to the marquee, environmental health wouldn't have it. We must persuade her to move elsewhere. Gwen, quickly, ring Billy and tell him we need him.'

Gwen glances at Ian, knowing they are beaten - for now at least - and makes for the office. Ian follows sorrowfully behind.

Nigel stops shovelling, and I stop barking, but Kate continues, she is enjoying herself too much! I lie on the cool, fresh soil and pant. Nigel looks down at me, smiles and makes for his Land Rover. Then he stops and looks back.

'I'll tell Billy to finish it, though the fox may be gone by the time he gets here'. He smiles again and walks on.

Kate and I are back in the cottage, trying to clear the last of the soil from our paws. Kate looks up and says,

'I'm sorry, you were right, there is some wickedness going on.'

I know Kate is talking about Ian and Gwen, but the thought jogs a memory and I tell her about Joe's cap; about it being in the same pattern of tweed as the body. I should have told her before. I tried to, but did she hear? And are these linked: Joe and Ian, Joe and the tweed, the tweed and the body? Everything seems to lead back to Joe…where will it finish? So many thoughts are rotating in my head. I look up for a response from Kate but see the last of her tail disappearing from the room and I don't know whether she heard me.

I settle into a deep sleep and am dreaming. I am down by the river in the line with Nigel, and I think we are somewhere near the middle. It is late in the season, a time when different guests come, and the birds are strong and wise. The drive is well on, and I can see birds rising in front. I am just wondering if they will fly this way, when I hear a shot that I wasn't expecting. A bird has come from the side, high and fast, and Nigel has hit but not killed it. It flies on, losing height, but determined to reach the wood, a distance to our right.

I am after it. The wood is very thick, and I know that if the bird gets there, I will struggle to find it, so I run at top speed. My eyes are glued on the bird and its eyes are glued on the wood. At last, I see it will touch down a few metres short of the wood and I am just a short distance behind, but I am exhausted. And so, with all my remaining energy, I dive at where I think it will land. We collide in a twisting mass of bodies and the air is full of feathers, soil and grass. We hit the fence that runs by the wood with an almighty crash. The bird hopes I will release my grip, but I don't and, as the air clears, I walk slowly to Nigel with my prize. I pass several other dogs on my way and pretend not to notice them. They will have seen my retrieve and that's what matters.

Why did I have this dream? Is it a need to hang on to what has always mattered to me? A need to remember something that I have always been good at, while everything else is so confusing?

We are about to host another wedding. The flower van is unloading and Steve, the chef, must be avoided at all costs. I have just dodged a most undeserved kick for innocently looking in the kitchen door. How was I to know he had just knocked over a large pan of soup? And even Jane has no time for me as she scampers by, looking for a child's bed that hasn't been used since New Year. I think of running after her as I know where it is, but then Nigel calls.

Kate is in the Land Rover, and Billy looks out of the window as I hop up. We head for the farm and the wild country beyond. It's good to be here, and away from the chaos at the castle. Kate and I stand on the old sack, I smile at her, and she smiles back; happy times are here again!

I wonder if Nigel really needs us, or has he been asked to take us out of the way? Whatever the reason, it gives me a chance to show Kate the estate for the first time since she's been here. She is relaxing, I can see it in her face. It's a look I haven't seen for so long and was afraid I wouldn't see again.

We stop on the track, exactly where Nigel stopped when I first saw the body. The waters have dried up, and only flattened rushes and scattered debris show where it has been. As Nigel and Billy drift into one of their eternal chats, Kate and I slip down the hill. We go through the overgrown hedge that separates the grazing field from the bottom area that is sometimes flooded and sometimes dry, but always wild and cloaked with rushes.

'There is no way it could have been washed here,' Kate says after a few short minutes. 'If the flood had reached right to the hedge, perhaps, but as it only came to here…' - she is looking at a fine line that shows clearly down the valley - '…No, definitely not!'

'So, how did it get here?' I ask, determined to make the most of her positive mood. Kate has walked out beyond where the body had been, she is looking for something.

'Mutley, do you remember the shoot before Christmas, when I retrieved a bird that had been washed down here.'

I nod.

'Well, was the water then similar to the day of your body.'

I think and then reply, 'Yes, very similar and certainly no higher. It hasn't been right to the hedge since last autumn.'

'Well, the pheasant finished up here', she says, and walks to a spot where a thistle is pushing its way between two young rushes. 'So how could something as big as a man be carried right over to you?'

I hear Nigel calling and make to return. Kate has wandered downstream. Is she scenting something; hasn't she heard Nigel? She is now a hundred metres away and has disappeared behind a thorn bush. Nigel is shouting loudly now, and I am about to leave Kate to her work when she reappears with something in her mouth, something she is struggling to carry. Nigel takes it from her and looks at it. It's a large leather cartridge bag.

8

Sophie arrives at lunch time. She has long, blonde, curly hair, two parents and a brother, much taller than her. I'm in the cottage and see her as she comes to her stables room, the one in the corner. I push open the cottage door, cross the courtyard and am waiting when she comes out. Her brother is pleased to see me, but Sophie is unsure and turns to her mother, hugging her.

I lead the way, back through the passage towards the castle, and the party follow. Sophie is in her mother's arms but with eyes fixed on me. I run onto the lawn and invite them to follow, and soon Sophie is crying to be put down. We run across to my underground tree camp and play. As she laughs, I glance towards the marquee, to the heap of soil that marks the phantom fox earth, and smile. I am happy now, but for how long? We still need to discover what Ian and Gwen are about before it's too late!

The wedding is small, with few guests and no one in the marquee. The food is served in the dining room at the top of the stairs and the girls carry it past me as I lie on the landing.

I glimpse Sophie through the open doorway; she sees me and calls. I wait till the girls have gone back downstairs, then creep through, hiding under the table by Sophie's knees. She smiles with joy and wickedness. We both know I shouldn't be there, but soon everyone in the room knows because Sophie tells them. Still, no one tries to move me, so I just lie there and eat the food that Sophie passes down.

I start to relax. Children have always been important to me. They seldom lie and, when they do, I know it but it's over little things that don't matter. I remember sitting under this same table with Kate when Joe ate his last supper here. It was the evening we saw the dog fox, and no one knew who the body was. I feel the smile leaving my face, till Sophie nudges me with another piece of chicken and returns me to her happy place.

You may be thinking, what have I done with Kate? Why hasn't she been helping with the wedding - has she taken to her bed again? No, Kate is well and, for the first time, has shown some interest in the wedding. I know that for a fully trained working dog, of which Kate is a prime example, something like a wedding is totally alien. She will be used to using her instinct to do a job that is very specialist, whereas a wedding requires a much more flexible and tolerant approach. Many have been amazed that I can carry out my wedding responsibilities and also be a prime working dog when needed.

Gwen has driven off and Nigel looks unhappy. Neither were here for the wedding and I'm afraid I've missed something to do with the new house. I know where she wants it to be. We drove by it last week when we showed Paul (the man with the dog called Trudy) the valley, and again just a few days ago. It is beyond the farm buildings on a bend of the road and looks down on a small valley with Boundary Hill in the distance. It is a lovely place, and where Nigel grows one of his best cover crops for pheasants. Was this the cause of the fiasco in the office when Kate sent me there to save the day? Was Gwen trying to commit Nigel to a new house?

Nigel takes me out to the Land Rover, and I know we are heading for this very spot. It's just brown soil, waiting to be planted when it's warm enough. We stand and look about. Nigel strokes me, telling me he doesn't want a house here and doesn't want to lose the crop, both of which are true. But when he looks at me, we both know that what he really means is he doesn't want Gwen, and that is the hardest problem of all.

Nigel parks the Land Rover under the old chestnut tree, below the main car park and a few metres from the chapel. He opens the vehicle door, and something falls out; it is the cartridge bag that Kate found in the valley. He hasn't noticed, so I let him stride away, his thoughts focused on some distant place. I pick up the bag and take it to my cedar tree; I'll give it to him later.

It's an old bag and made of light-coloured leather, but it's darker where it's been on the ground and the dampness has soaked in. The strap carries an unusual pattern, a tartan with a dominant orange stripe. Inside are a few bright yellow shotgun cartridges, which are still dry, dry enough to use. How long was it there? I must ask Kate exactly where she found it.

I know this bag with its awful orange stripe; it belongs to Hamish, the team captain who made the speech. When was that, was it Christmas? Yes! But then I remember they had their Christmas meal at the end of their final day, and that was after Christmas, after I had found the body.

I think of the day, and remember how the sun had shone, how the birds didn't want to fly and how grumpy Billy had become. The thought makes me smile and I long for the next season, a time when my life might make sense again. But can I remember the bag? Did Hamish have it that day? He must have.

I close my eyes and try to return to the sporting season, to get my mind back into gear. It doesn't take long. Hamish and his party never shoot down by the river. They never stand anywhere near where Kate found the bag - the birds fly too high, the challenge would be too great! I nudge the bag with a paw, as if this might make it tell me its story and help solve the mystery. How could it have been left where Kate found it? Hamish had no reason to go there. What has it to do with the body? Why did the police miss it?

Kate comes out and joins me, and we scratch out the worst of the winter debris from under the cedar tree to make a nice patch to lie. I have pushed the bag behind me, there will be time enough later for that.

'You would have liked Gunner', I say to Kate, thinking of the old dog in whose memory the neighbouring tree was planted and whose bare branches are taking my attention. 'He wasn't good with fools or postmen either!'

Kate laughs. 'What have I ever done to postmen?'

It's so good to laugh again, to glimpse the old Kate and, although I must, I'm very reluctant to ask my next question.

'What do you make of Tim? I know he worries you.'

I roll onto my side to find a more comfortable position. We know he's home, but I've only seen him briefly and we didn't get a chance to speak, while Kate hasn't seen him at all. How can she have an answer? Yet I know she does and wants to tell me.

'He's dying, and it won't be long, but you know that,' she says, not quite meeting my eyes.

I find myself nodding a reply, but I want to stop. How is he dying and why? How can Kate say this without having seen him? Yet the way she speaks and looks tells me she is right.

'So', I venture, 'the cloud told you of his collapse and, because it hasn't gone away, you think it tells of his death too.'

'Yes, at least that', she says, with frightening confidence. 'There may be others.'

'Others?', I splutter.

She hesitates. 'I don't know.' She can see I'm shocked but can't stop now. 'Tim makes everything so dark. I can't make out if it's all for him, or if some is for those around him.'

She lies back and sighs, as if just thinking about it exhausts her. I see why she has been so odd lately, what has been troubling her.

'Tim is easy to see', she continues. 'He needs all our love, and we can give him that. No, what is really troubling me is the huge cloud that is there - it seems too big for one person.'

My confusion shows on my face. She looks at me in a way she never has before, with fear and disbelief.

'I think Tim may be just the tip of the iceberg!'

Nigel hears from Paul today, and yes, he is bringing his party to have a day with us in December. When he tells me, I instantly remember that his dog is called Trudy, but I can't picture her. I can't even remember what breed she is! I know I've been leading a hectic life and Kates's talk of 'tips of icebergs', has thrown me, but this is unforgiveable. Kate walks up and whispers in my ear,

'Golden cocker.'

I look at her, aghast. I hadn't discussed that day with her. She is reading my mind again!

She returns to the cottage, and I decide she needs more quiet time to regain her strength, so I go to find Nigel.

🐾

We have stopped at a point along the top road between two woods. Nigel is surrounded by sheep, so I have left him to it and am thinking of Tim. I can still see the bright, tall, fit young man who threw a ball so far, and my mind can't find room for the well-wrapped person who sits as a pheasant would in a game cart. Is Kate right, is he going to die? She seems so sure. When we get back, I will visit him. I will talk to him and make up my own mind.

The wind is growing stronger and, again, it's from the east. I sense a change that makes me shiver. We return to the castle, and I hop down from the Land Rover and push under the hedge into Tim's garden. I scratch on the door until Sarah comes and lets me in. I think she's expecting me. There is no surprise in her eyes, and she leads me straight to Tim's room. The face is the face that has always been Tim's, but the life has gone from it, and when I stand in front of him, he only manages a slight smile. His arm moves a little and I walk below it, brushing his hand along my back. I want him to grip me, but his hand just hangs like a branch on my cedar tree. I curl up as close to him as I can, hoping I bring him some comfort.

In the morning it's snowing again. My tree camp is filling with blown snow and more has slipped from the marquee roof and turned the troughs of flowers that looked so good at the fair into a huge drift with not a single petal visible.

I love snow; it feels so soft between my paws and the taste of it first thing in the morning is better than any water. It's good for rabbits too. It keeps them in their burrows for a while, especially the young ones who haven't seen it before, but when they venture out, I can see them more easily and always feel I will catch one. Sometimes I have cornered them, but they can turn faster than me and seem to be laughing as they disappear underground.

Nigel is standing by the front door as a police car arrives, and I run to meet them, to hear the news. The snow has nearly stopped falling, but the policemen are reluctant to leave the warmth of their car. Nigel walks to them, carrying the bag that Kate found. I had left it by the front desk, and I don't think he knew he had dropped it. At last, they get out, climb into the Land Rover, and Kate and I are called too. We are going to the spot where Kate found the bag, though what good it will do I don't know; nothing will look the same after the snow! Nigel makes to walk down the field, but the policemen decline his offer and ask him to simply point out where it was. They nod, though their view will have been blocked by the thick thorn hedge and we can see Nigel is as unimpressed as we are. We return to the castle, the policemen drive off, carrying the bag, and Nigel retreats indoors. I look at Kate and give a wry smile; I know what the bag may mean, even if the policemen don't!

🐾

Thoughts of the bag want to occupy my mind, but the busy comings and goings in the castle finally destroy any hope of real rest or concentration. Cars make their way down the slushy drive for most of the morning, and the arrival of each one means the opening of the door and a blast of cold air.

'Enough is enough', I decide, as an even colder blast freezes me into action. I want to be angry, but realise that, amongst the usual bags of clothes and papers, are an array of packages carrying pictures of happy dogs and smelling very good indeed.

I know we hold what are called 'conferences' from time to time. I have taken little interest. They are mainly held behind closed doors and, when guests do walk outside, they spend their time talking to themselves with small boxes held firmly against an ear.

A guest throws a stone for me, but it disappears into the remnants of the snow, and he turns away, laughing. I am mystified by the packages. Outside, among the cars, is a van with the same picture of a happy dog standing out brightly on a darker background and with its rear door open. I need to investigate.

I walk briskly across the drive and find the van driver talking merrily to the girl in the next car. I sniff inside the van and find myself almost faint with the intensity of the smell. People seldom realise that dogs have a much better and more acute sense of smell than they do. We can gain many joys they can't, such as the richness of a spring morning, a pheasant trying to creep away through thick winter undergrowth – and the back of this van! It also means that people don't have to suffer bad smells as we do, which is a poor excuse for the way they often live. Anyway, I am determined to know what has created such a wonderful aroma.

My mind is full of roast beef, perhaps some rabbit and I'm sure there is some sausage in there too, and why the pictures of happy dogs? The guests walk upstairs, and I follow. They settle in the dining room, the large room on the first floor where Sophie's wedding party ate their meal, and they leave the door open. I sit on the landing and listen to what they say. They talk about 'pets', and I soon realise they mean animals, at least, those animals who live with people. This, I can see, includes me and I listen with keener interest, but much of what they say is about money. I do hope they return to more important matters shortly.

I hear Nigel calling my name from downstairs and stand up to answer. Why does nothing of great interest seem to happen for days and then several matters needing my attention come together? Whatever Nigel wants had better be very important, I think, very important indeed! And it is. We are going to the Home Farm – not to shoot, but to see how the place looks as spring approaches, and to make plans for next season.

I love travelling by car, though I seldom get the chance. I love to sit on the passenger seat and poke my nose out of the partially open window, to feel the wind in my fur and sense my ears blown back against my neck. Kate is beside me and seems fascinated in her calm, unflustered way. She hasn't been here when the hen pheasants are laying their eggs, and everything is making ready for the new season. I can't sit still, and she must sense how important all this is, yet she just sits and looks and takes it in, with little excitement in her eyes.

When we arrive, we see Billy is carrying eggs to his incubator in the old barn. In the field behind his house, he's building pens ready for the young birds. Bill is in his kennel, so I wander over and talk to him while the men speak. The snow is thawing fast and trickling from the old slate roof. Another dog comes and looks at me through the bars of his kennel. It's the new dog, the one I've called Ben. Billy lets Bill out and Kate joins him on a circuit of the field. I stay where I am because I want to speak to the new dog and find out if he has remembered anything since we last met. He is still scared of Billy, cowering to the side as the next tray of pheasant eggs is carried past, but as peace returns, he looks at me. He seems more relaxed and wants to talk.

He tells me that his master was a guest on the day. That, at the end of it, they returned to the valley as the snow fell to look for a bird that had come down earlier. Ben says he hunted fruitlessly, but then found a scent that took him a good distance up the hedge line. He returned to find his master motionless on the ground, a bird in his hand. Everything was silent, deathly silent. He was shocked and, in many ways, still is!

Ben starts to walk away, head down, but then turns and says,

'Why does Billy shout so much?'

I can't give him an answer but promise I will tell Nigel that he is a good dog and maybe he can help. Ben's memory is slowly improving. If I am patient, perhaps he will recall more about that terrible day. So, as I expected, my body died where he fell; where I found him. And was it just an accident, as the police seem to think? I just can't see how such an accident could happen in that spot. I walk around to meet Kate and Bill.

There are pheasants here, not just the old hen birds with their husbands in the laying pens, but visiting cock birds, who walk around outside hoping to find a mate. I reach the corner, and three run in front of me, now trapped by the wire fence. I think of running at them and making them fly - it would certainly ease my frustration - but decide it would be too easy, so I warn them not to tempt me and wander on.

We get back in the Land Rover and drive on from the yard and up to one of the top woods. Most of it is thick and dark and the snow is still lying. Billy and Nigel walk into the wood and I lie down beside Kate.

'Ben told me that yes, he was with the man who became the body.' I recount the tale as Ben told it to me. Kate nods, and then replies,

'So, he was killed where you found him; I have decided he had to be. All we must do now is find who did it and why!'

Kate clearly wants to link the deaths, my body and Joe. She has dismissed the idea of them being accidents and is she right? For that we may have to wait on her 'cloud'.

Nigel and Billy have come out of the wood and are standing on a flat area which would be a good spot for a new cover crop. I could make the birds fly from here, or the rest of the team could, and I could wait with Nigel at the bottom to retrieve the birds. But Nigel and Billy decide the wood is too dark, and that few birds would enjoy living in so dismal a place, so we drive on to find somewhere better. We arrive at another wood and, straight away, I am thinking of the next season. I scent pheasants and am drawn to a bush growing by a dead spruce tree. It is warm and bright, and a cock bird runs away, calling for his wives in a loud voice.

From the edge of the wood, I look down into the valley and my mind is back with what Ben has told me. Kate moves beside me.

'It was just out from that oak tree,' she says, without varying her gaze. It looks different from this angle, but she is right. The body must have been about there. I let my eyes follow the river upstream to the loch, and to the spot the police think the body floated from. I look again at the meadow, at the oak and then at some tracks above it. Most of the snow has gone, melting quickly, and only remains in hollows, contrasting with the bare, green ground around it. At the far end, a group of pheasants is just a few yards from the hedge, and I imagine them soaring over the valley, but my attention is with the tracks. The more I look, the clearer they become, highlighted by the snow still clinging to the impressions the tracks have made. They come down from the rutted road, and then return to it.

Why hadn't I noticed these tracks before? How do they fit in with what Ben has said and with everything Kate and I have suspected?

9

We have returned from our trip up the valley and the conference has finished. The guests are either drinking in the bar or, true to form, talking to themselves outside. I wander slowly. What have I missed? Kate soon appreciates the smell coming from the van, but it is now locked and deserted, so we return to reception and lie on my sofa. We want to solve the mystery of the happy dogs, even more because it comes as welcome relief from the mystery of the tracks. That is a mystery we must solve, but dread what it will tell us. I don't like to be beaten by a mystery and think of teasing Kate about her inability to 'see' an answer.

I must have dozed off, because I'm woken by Kate, Jane and a lady that I recognise as one of the guests, and who comes holding two of the mystery packages. It is a present; a brightly coloured bag of some of the tastiest dog food I have ever eaten. It does not compare, of course, with fillet steak after a wedding, or rich beef stew after a sporting lunch, but a treat is a treat after all!

I have taken my thoughts to a sheltered spot behind the marquee, where the daffodils are appearing as yellow spears reaching towards the sky. Nigel walks across the lawn and looks at the ground, pushing down with his foot,

'Will it mow?' I hear him say.

It won't, I know, as only this morning I dug for rabbits near my cedar tree and the soil is still firmly stuck between my paws. He tries not to believe me, but soon sees I'm right. He throws his head back in annoyance and goes to his office. I look through the hedge into Tim's garden, where he is sitting, wrapped in a light blanket. I go to him, and as I look into his eyes, they speak to me.

He tells me he has been to the hospital twice since I last saw him. He is going again tomorrow and is very bored; bored and scared. If he can tell me all this without speaking, I must be able to tell him all that I have been doing too. I will only tell him the funny and happy bits. I want to make him laugh inside, and so I start.

He has never been out on a sporting day, so when I describe it, I must make sure I give him enough detail that he can picture it. I tell him about the beautiful loch at the top of the valley, with the high sides climbing up to where the peregrine nests. I tell him of the river that descends from it and of the meadows and woods it runs through. It is difficult for me not to mention some of the times that have made this place so special to me, and I fear I'm boring him, but I see he is excited by the same bits that excite me, so I continue. I don't know how long I go on, but I notice his eyes have shut. As I am beginning to worry, he opens them again and I know he is just very tired.

I squeeze my way back under the fence, Kate is waiting for me on her bed beside the Aga. I want to ask why she didn't join us, but her eyes tell me. She is scared too; scared of what Tim's illness might mean.

'I didn't realise you needed so many hen pheasants', she says. 'But thinking about it, I suppose you do.'

What's brought this on, I wonder? She hasn't mentioned the trip since we got back.

'Billy likes to have plenty; then he can release them in good time when he has enough eggs, and they can have a clutch of their own,' I reply.

Kate nods, showing she sees the logic of this, then rolls over in the way that tells me she has nothing more to say. I long to know what she really thinks. Is she really interested in Billy's hen pheasants or is she just trying to relax, to help me relax? She saw the vehicle tracks highlighted by the retreating snow just as I did, and both of us knew their importance.

🐾

Nigel is in his office. I think he's putting our visit up the valley on to the computer; he loves that thing! I venture out into the early spring sunshine and hear Peter, the handyman, working behind the marquee. When I go there, I see the snowdrops are dying off, but that bright, yellow-green, leaves are breaking out from the sad, drooping branches of the lime trees. It's warmer here, and a blackbird hops across the lawn in front of me looking for worms drawn up by the sun. I recognise her as the one who nests in the bush by my scraggy pine. A few days like this and everything will change; real spring will arrive!

Yes, it's a quiet and particularly beautiful morning when Nigel emerges from his office and walks across the gardens. He looks at the trees and shrubs that are spread out in front of us; at how they are thriving or otherwise. As he comes to the young trees that have been planted amongst the tall limes, he becomes unusually quiet, and I can see why. Several of them have been chewed around their base and will probably die. One catches my eye; it's the young tree that marks old Gunner's grave. It has been badly chewed. He says nothing, he doesn't need to. I am fully aware that I have been negligent in my rabbit control duties, and this is the evidence. He gives me a single glance and I know nothing more will be said or done.

I think of Tim and of him being 'the tip of the iceberg'. I cross the drive and push under the fence, but he's not there. Sarah is watching from their sitting room; she slides open the patio doors and beckons me. Tim is in the chair with the best view of the garden and he knows I am coming. What can I say? Kate's cloud has filled me with fear and made me want to stay away. How can I look him in the eye when I've let him down so? But when I do look up at his face, I see only love and thanks, fighting their way through the pain that is so much worse than it was. I run over to him and lie on his feet, nestling my chin on his leg. I don't know if he can feel it, but he knows I am there and how sorry I am.

When I return to the cottage, Kate is waiting. She has clearly been letting the vision of the vehicle tracks work in her mind. She leads me out to the cedar tree.

'So, we now know the body was driven down the field, and then carried to the edge of the water and left there.' Kate says.

'I considered this conclusion too, but it doesn't explain how the pheasant was still clasped in the hand, or the story that Ben told me', I reply.

'You're right; they must have driven and carried the body there, then put the pheasant in the hand after, though for what reason?'

'Or they drove him down and killed him there', I add. 'Or perhaps the tracks have nothing to do with the body, and its death was just an accident.'

Kate looks at me with a we-have-said-all-this-before look.

'No, the tracks are to do with the body, as are the other little points that may mean a lot.'

I look at her. 'What little points?'

The old, exasperated look returns.

'Oh, just the question of why I found the cartridge bag some hundred metres from the body? Why someone put a dead pheasant into the body's hand and what happened to the pheasant that Ben was retrieving whilst the murder was being committed?'

She pauses; 'Unless you retrieved that too and haven't mentioned it.'

I don't appreciate that comment and hope I show it.

'No, Ben didn't find his bird, at least, he hasn't said he did; and the bag belonged to Hamish, the shoot captain of the team that can't shoot straight!'

The exasperated look has gone, and the meaning of my words slowly sinks in. She looks up into the air and says, 'Got it!'

🐾

'Gwen's gone to see her mother, you can fill her shifts for the week', Ian says, obviously speaking to Jane, though I hear no answer.

I have been wondering where Gwen had gone, and I doubt it's to see her mother. I find myself disbelieving everything Ian or Gwen say. My mind drifts back to Kate's account of

Joe's first meeting with Ian at the castle. We still don't know where Joe recognised him from, but it must be relevant – and so must Gwen's wish to marry Nigel. Oh, I do wish things were clearer!

I want to have a go at the rabbits with Freddy, a visiting terrier, who is the companion of an elderly lady called Maud. I know Kate has more important things on her mind. Whether it's from yesterday's conversation about the body, or her 'cloud', I don't know; but if I could persuade her to join us, we might have some real effect. I think of asking her, but then remember I don't need to. She seems to know just what I'm doing and when.

And I'm right! Kate appears, keen to join us for the rabbiting, and we go to the thick area at the top of the drive. I guard the escape route back to the field.

I glance across the valley and look for Nigel. He's been away all day, and I sense he needs me. As I am looking, a rabbit runs straight past me with Freddie in full pursuit, showing surprising speed to add to his high-pitched voice. The rabbit ducks into its burrow beneath a heap of old stones and Freddie scratches at it, but when he sees the stones are solid, he turns away. As he returns, he comments that it should have been my job to catch it. He's right. I must concentrate on the job.

The day is nearly over, and I still haven't found Nigel. I realise I haven't seen Sarah either, and when Oliver comes in from his shift in the lambing yard, I know they must be together. Freddy has gone, sitting meekly beside Maud in her old red car and we have caught nothing!

And now Kate is missing. In fact, everyone seems to be missing, except Jane, who is at the reception desk and Peter, the handyman, whom I found moving boxes. I stand by the front door wondering where Kate could be, and then I see a movement under the cedar tree. I should have known - there is nowhere better to escape the world than this weeping tree.

I run over and Kate seems pleased to see me. Her eyes have a sparkle I haven't seen for several weeks and between her paws something else sparkles. I'm about to ask what it is when she speaks.

'I'm sure it's not just Tim', she says, looking towards Tim's garden. 'Have you noticed that his illness has grown slightly worse in the last few weeks?'

I had been trying to convince myself that he is improving, or at least holding his own, but when she puts it so bluntly, I can't disagree. I look at the rabbit-scarred tree trunk nearby and softly reply, 'Yes.'

'Well, if he was getting much nearer to the end and he's the cause of my cloud, the cloud that I see over him should be intensifying too.'

She says this with an undue degree of cheerfulness and immediately sees I am not impressed.

'Don't you understand, Mutley, that I only see things clearly when they are about to happen. I can't look very far ahead.'

My expression of disapproval has turned to one of confusion and she sighs her annoyance.

'If Tim is the cause of what I am calling my 'cloud', then his nearness to death would cause the cloud to intensify – and it's not.'

I finally understand. 'So, he may not be dying; it might be a temporary decline that the next trip to hospital could put right. If he were close to death, you would have seen it.'

'Yes', she starts, but then she hesitates. 'It could mean just that.' She pauses and swallows. 'Or it could be that he is dying, and the cloud is not to do with him at all, but with something else that is still to come.'

I don't listen to the end of her statement. Tim isn't going to die, I tell myself. He isn't going to die!

I didn't sleep that night, and even tried to blame Kate's snoring for keeping me awake. Tim will live! The thought echoes in my head. As I lie, listening to the steady moan of the Aga that seems so quiet during the day, I finally realise what Kate is trying to say. She believes Tim is still going to die and that this cloud of hers signifies something else important that will happen, but not for a little while. Yes, I'm sure that's what she means. Anyway, the two things that seem most important in the dark hours of the night are that Tim might live and that nothing drastic is to happen, yet!

As light begins to peep through the kitchen window, I am ready to help Tim on his road to recovery. Despite the sound of heavy rain hitting the glass, I close my eyes and tell myself that when I open them it will be the hottest and sunniest day of the year. And, as with most heavy rain, it doesn't last long and soon the sun I wished for calls me outside.

I pretend to patrol the hotel grounds. The rain has brought a wonderful freshness to everything, and the smell of growth is almost overpowering – but not enough to dislodge the strong smell of rabbits! And yet, this morning they could dance in my face, and I would dance with them. Their day will come; today is Tim's.

He is away, back in hospital, but even this can't dampen my mood. It is a sign that his cure has started, I tell myself, and I look to his return and my part in his recovery. Kate finds me under the hedge and asks me to follow. I know she notices my cheeriness but is choosing to ignore it. She leads me up the drive towards the road, and then to the right and to where Freddie's rabbit went underground. She scratches away a few stones that guard the entrance, and something glistens, shining through the mud and soil. I rush to her side, and we both scratch frantically with our paws, but the stones are solid, like an underground wall. A ring, a dented cup and a bracelet have appeared, but we can glimpse more.

'It's no good', Kate finally admits. 'We will have to cover them up until we can think of a way in. And we can put what we do have in your camp – no one but you ever goes there!'

She smiles with the brilliance of her idea. She is her old self again, at least for now. Whether it's the excitement of her find, coming to terms with her 'cloud', or other thoughts she hasn't shared with me yet, doesn't matter. It's taken a weight off her shoulders, and I want us to enjoy it.

The road seems especially bumpy, and the vehicle especially hard as we drive towards the farm. I hope we are going on, through the buildings and up the valley to the loch, or the moorland, or one of the woods that stands between them, but we turn off by a large barn and stop. Nigel gets out and walks into the barn.

All I can smell is sheep. Metal gates, feed troughs, bales of straw and hundreds of sheep fill my view and my nose! I hate sheep. They have rarely been the best friend of pheasant keeper or working dog, always trying to take grain from the feeders or break through the fence to graze the cover crops. But my true hatred came when Archie, a terrier I knew and loved, chased a tiny sheep that could easily have been mistaken for a large rabbit. I will always blame them for his departure.

Kate and I stay in the Land Rover and watch as Nigel talks with Oliver, while John, the shepherd, feeds the sheep. I notice Kate is asleep and, across the yard, John is walking away.

Oliver is crying, and Nigel is sitting on an old chair, looking at him. They are drinking coffee from old, chipped mugs, and the kettle is steaming on a makeshift table covered with more medicines than Billy would use in a season. Nigel puts his arm around Oliver. I haven't seen Oliver for a while, and I know he is ill, but why is he crying? Is it over Tim? It makes me curl up and feel very sad, till I remember that Tim is going to recover. I want to leap out and tell Oliver it is going to be all right!

Another day dawns, and I am still trying to tell myself that Kate is wrong about Tim while helping Gwen with a wedding show-round. Ian is on holiday and Jane is busy at the desk. Gwen can certainly turn on the charm when required, and the young couple seem enthralled by her. We are in the drive of the castle, and Gwen is reminding the guests to confirm their booking promptly as days are going fast. As they drive away, her radiant smile disappears, and she strides past me as if I wasn't there.

I am wondering whether I should return indoors or patrol the lawns, when Kate runs up, wanting me to follow. Behind the lake, she stops by a rabbit burrow and pretends to sniff, and then moves on to my camp and slides in; one glance tells her the treasure is still secure.

'Just because I haven't foreseen Tim's death doesn't mean he will recover. You know that, don't you?'

I pretend to sniff some imaginary scent and then reply, 'Yes, I do, but he may, and if we want it enough, perhaps he will!'

Kate grunts as though she understands my words, but not my logic, and makes to return to the lakeside.

'And are you any nearer seeing the true cause of your latest cloud?', I shout after her. The words come out more sarcastically than I intend, and she swings round angrily.

'This isn't a trivial thing you know. It's not a game! Have you forgotten that my last cloud led to Joe's death?'

'No, I'm sorry, of course I haven't, but surely this one is different?' I look at her, willing her to agree.

'Yes, I think it might be', she says. 'When the event gets nearer, the cloud will strengthen, and its true meaning will become clear.'

'So, how long are you saying; a day, a week, a month, a year?'

I think I sound sarcastic again and for a while she doesn't respond. Then I see she is asking herself for an answer. Eventually she turns and looks me straight in the eye.

'More than a month, I think, but less than a year, and don't ask me for more details, I don't have any.'

She seems annoyed, but who with? Me for asking, or herself for not knowing. She walks a few feet away, then stops and says, more kindly,

'You have plenty of time to wish Tim well.'

10

Tim has been back in hospital and I'm sure it's the best place for him to start his recovery. That belief is something I want, need to hang on to. I wonder how I can help him when he seems so far away. I walk my lawns as the sun sets and look through his hedge, wishing him well.

The next morning has broken with a special sun shining and I sense Tim is home. He must have come back late last night. I rush to his door and Sarah lets me in. How much better will he be? He's sitting in a chair beside his bed and I'm looking at his feet and the odd socks he's wearing, at his hands and the way they are hanging by his side. Since my arrival a few minutes ago, I have looked everywhere but at his face, because faces don't lie. He will know the confidence I have in his recovery is unsure, my faith is uncertain. Does he really look better, or is it just that I want him to?

Part of me wants to share Kate's worries with him. Not the whole 'cloud' thing, of course - I know he's not strong enough for that - just something for him to work on that will show his mind is alive! But, as I look into his eyes, I think, not yet. In the end, I just lie by his feet and will him to get better.

When I'm sure he's asleep I wander outside. Nigel stops his lawn mowing, everything becomes wonderfully silent, and the birds start to sing. Perhaps they want to help me, to help Tim? I walk on to my tree camp and push the shiny cup and bracelet further under the roots. I hear the doves calling in the tree behind me and then my blackbird, answering from a branch just above my head. I run my paw over the ring and cup. What is it and where is it from? I sense it is important, but how? An idea starts to form, but then the beauty is destroyed, Nigel has restarted his mower. I lay my paws over my ears and try to rest.

Eventually I succeed but am soon woken by a car squealing its brakes, then turning and speeding down the drive. It's Gwen. I know she returned yesterday from supposedly seeing her mother, I wonder where she's been now. She leaps from her car and rushes into the castle. I think she's looking for Nigel but know she won't find him; I heard him leave the mower and go up the valley with Billy a couple of minutes ago. Never mind, I think, I am sure you can wait!

A day has passed and I'm with Nigel. We are back by the rearing pens, the ones behind the old barn, and Nigel and Billy are talking. They are at the far side, so I don't hear what they're saying, and they can't see me. Kate was with them but has grown tired of their chatter and I saw her go towards Ben's kennel.

'Have you learnt anything interesting?' I ask, as she returns. 'Has Ben anything to add to what he told me?'

She faces me. 'I pushed him on the silence. If his story is right and he found his master on the ground, the murder could only just have happened. Why didn't he hear the murderer escaping, a vehicle climbing up the slope?'

I look at her, and a chilling thought crosses my mind.

'Unless the murderer was still there, lurking in the hedgerow? If Ben is to be believed, the murder took place where I found the body, and was committed by the person driving the vehicle.'

It's Kate's turn to nod.

I continue, 'And did Ben have anything to add; some vital point that will lead us to the killer? Did he hear a vehicle at all? Is he deaf?'

Kate clearly has more facts to tell me, but then shakes her head, as though she's not sure how to proceed. I'm sure she just needs a moment to gather her thoughts, so I wait. Sure enough, after a short while, she takes a deep breath and says,

'We know that the dead man was in a party that was here five days before he was found, but that he was not missed during the day.'

I nod agreement. I admire her logic, though I still can't see where she's going.

'If he was killed where you found him, perhaps he had come there at the end of the day to look for a wounded bird, as you or I might.'

'Just as Ben says he did.' I add.

Kate nods again and smiles. 'The bird was safely in the man's hand when the murderer struck. And he was down before Ben returned, so Ben must have found a second bird.'

'Or the man had found the first and only bird and Ben had been on a false scent,' I add quickly. 'Or the bird in his hand was put there by the killer to say something, to send a message!'

'No,' Kate interrupts. 'None of these add up! If the murderer wanted it to look like an accident, with the body floating down stream to where you found him, he wouldn't leave a bird in his hand, would he?'

'No, and I suppose if one was already there when he struck, he would surely have removed it.'

Kate nods, 'Just as you did for him before the police could see the body. So, if the bird was there, why didn't the murderer take it?'

It doesn't add up.

'We need to find out who drove down leaving the tracks; was it our victim or the murderer?' Kate adds energetically, feeling we are getting somewhere at last.

'Whoever killed him must have known where to find him and when - or the tracks are to do with something else', I say.

'No', replies Kate. 'As I've said, I don't believe in coincidence! But there was only one set of tracks, so either the killer drove down, or the man drove and the killer walked there.'

'Or they both drove down together!', I add, before she can get the words out. One look and I see she thinks the same! We are getting nowhere again.

🐾

The sight of young birds and talk of the coming season affects me more than I like anyone to know. I have been occupied with the aftermath of Joe's death, the body and the effects of what Kate can, or sometimes can't see. We have gone from day to day without either of us having time to think much beyond that, and certainly not about any preparations for the coming season.

What part will Kate play? How will it affect my responsibilities? She has shown no interest in helping with the work around the castle; will the sporting season be any different?

It is the hottest day of the year so far, the snow has completely gone and just the shortest run leaves me with my tongue out, panting for breath. While I hate the heat, Billy enjoys this weather for his young birds. He'll be hoping the rain doesn't start and forget to stop.

Back at the castle, I am still feeling sorry for myself when Richard, one of our regular sportsmen, turns up. His arrival cools me with thoughts of a frosty winter's morning. I can imagine the steam from my mouth hitting the icy breeze, and a new friend running excitedly beside me. I remember her as being small, with a shiny coat and the brightest eyes. Her name is Bess. Although Richard has been many times before, I only met Bess last year, when she was just two years old. I thought her very attractive but, as host, and with other dogs visiting at the time, I couldn't give her the attention I wanted to.

So, this time I'm happy we can creep away together, and I can tell her all about my estate (and, yes, I do exaggerate a little!). She has enjoyed a single season with her master and is keen to learn from me. I warn her about the cold, wet days when the work is hard, the birds are few, and the teasing of the other dogs who like nothing better than to make a young dog look silly and do all the work. But, having lowered her spirits, I try to raise them again with tales of courage and success that make it all worthwhile.

Later, while Nigel and Gwen join Richard for supper, Bess and I lie on my sofa, and I regale her some of my favourite stories. Everything I tell her is true, though as the evening draws on, I must admit, a little romance creeps into the telling.

Kate, who is lying nearby, is amused by my banter, sometimes smiling at my tales and occasionally letting out a little whimper as if to say,

'I can't believe you just said that!'

I relax in a way I haven't for so long, and happy memories return, which I share with Bess. You may remember that way back in January, I mentioned my fear of heights. This stemmed from a terrible day when it had rained all the previous night and well into the morning. All the ground was running with water and all the cover was saturated. At times like this, the birds do their best to hide in the thickest and driest cover - and who can blame them? - and, having hidden in as dry a spot as they can find, are very loath to leave. It takes all my determination to persuade them to move, and such was the case with a cock pheasant in a thick bramble bush at the top of a steep slope.

I knew he was there, his scent was strong, but it took several seconds before he moved and ran for the next bush. I ran as fast as I could and was determined to make him fly, which he did. However, he didn't fly forwards, as I wanted, but back and away from the waiting guests, and I think it was my annoyance at this that broke my concentration.

I failed to see the bank drop away sharply, just where he had taken off, and I fell. I thought I was going to fall for ever as I crashed through bushes and narrowly missed a tree. I came to rest in some rushes very near the river and lay there for a minute, regaining my breath. No one saw me, and it was only later, when Nigel noticed I had a cut on a leg, that he knew I had fallen. I didn't tell him the full story, he wouldn't have understood, and some things are best kept between dogs.

I can tell she is impressed and would probably have been more so without Kate's assistance. We share a late-night walk on the lawns, whilst Nigel and Richard sit on the old seat and watch their cigar smoke drift in the evening breeze. Just a few days ago the seat was covered with snow, but now the stars seem brighter than ever. It grows cold, but Kate, Bess and I settle under the garden table and, for now at least, all seems good with the world.

🐾

The ambulance is outside Tim's house and I'm worried. When it leaves, I lie down by the fence and wait. I don't know what I'm waiting for, or what to do, but I know Tim wants me there. It grows warm in the sun and soon I'm asleep. I hear a rustle beside me, and Kate is there. She doesn't say anything, just lies down and rests her chin on a paw. I want her to speak, to give me hope, but I know that silence is the best she can do.

In the middle of the afternoon, as I sit with Sarah on their lawn, I learn that Tim has had another operation. Sarah hopes it will make him better and, while I hope so too, I'm not sure.

The next day, Tim returns in the ambulance that sometimes means hope, and sometimes worry. He is very happy to see me, and I am pleased he seems in good spirits. I tell him about Bess and he teases me. He wants to know what Kate thinks about Bess because he likes Kate and wants us to stay together. I feel uncomfortable and decide to tell him the story I told Bess about my fall, as I know he likes action stories. How I long for many more days like this with Tim.

🐾

Tomorrow, the Saturday after Richard and Bess's departure, is another wedding. Most of those we host have very much in common, but this one is quite different.

Many of the guests arrive tonight, though the wedding is not until tomorrow. They eat dinner in the main dining room, dressed up in strange outfits - not in the usual dress that humans love wearing at weddings - and some are in bright colours. Nigel stands in front of them. He tells them they must pretend to be someone they are not, and he says that someone has been killed.

At first, I am worried and think that there is actually another dead body! I know that birds are killed on sporting days, but that seems very different to killing a guest. Fortunately, they are only pretending and the fun, I understand, is to work out which guest is best at pretending. This excites me. I have seen many guests claim to have been successful on a sporting day when I know they have missed completely. I think I am far more qualified to solve the crime than most who are taking part. They seem to listen to conversations and believe what they are told, when I can tell the murderer just by the look on their face.

Thoughts of murder return the image of my body to my mind – and especially the face that I still can't see. Tonight's entertainment makes me want it even more. Will the approaching season show it to me?

I wish my real mystery was as easy as this pretend one. I leave the party to their chatter and wander downstairs. After the noise of the dining room, the quiet here is wonderful. A guest goes outside, and I follow, but when he sits at the garden table I walk on across the lawn towards the lake. The lights around the water have come on now and shine across it, catching the ripples from the waterfall and fountain. The lake is one of my favourite parts of the garden and at night it has an extra beauty. I lie on the grass and listen to the frogs croaking and look at the lights of the castle shining out. Soon the guests will find their murderer, retire to the bar and, eventually, go to their beds. I drink at the water's edge; it is cool and refreshing! I rest my chin on my paws and close my eyes.

In the morning, children run everywhere, and in the evening, as the sun settles in a glowing sky, a full football match takes place. It involves most of the guests of all ages. I watch for a few minutes, and then join in. I have played before and find it much easier and more friendly than cricket, though I wish the ball was smaller. They use the whole lawn, right up to the lime trees, and my speed is too great for any of them. However, once I arrive at the ball, I have problems picking it up. Guests shout from all sides and, if I succeed, they shout louder - some even moan. Men have very selective humour sometimes and tonight, to avoid any unhappiness, I just pass the ball with my nose.

The game is now at the top of the lawn, and someone is trying to score by going behind a lime tree. I am resting under one of the garden tables and notice Gwen and Ian walk behind the lake. They will be scheming, I'm sure. I think of following them but know they would see me, and I don't want them to think of me as a risk.

As Sunday arrives, I could really do with a lie-in, but I don't get one. Nigel walks through with his coat in his hand, calling,

'Come on Mutley, come on Kate, we are going to look at some new country.'

We drive for half an hour, in roughly the same direction as another area I knew just a few years ago. I am confused. How will this 'new country' look and what will it mean for me? Because we are going in the same direction as the old place, I expect it to be similar. My memory is flooded with thoughts of pheasants and waterfalls, of big rocks and thick bushes.

When we arrive, I am amazed; it could not have been more different. Where the old place had been mainly grassland with trees in the valleys, this is almost treeless. Where it had neat grass fields, this is an open expanse of rough grass and heather, with no fences. In the single valley that runs through the middle of the ground stand just two trees, and these are stunted and bent by the wind. Nigel is surprised too.

I leave him and Billy talking and walk a little down the slope. I could say I am disappointed and, certainly, the absence of rabbits doesn't help, so I lie down to rest my weary legs, while the two men chat. Kate wanders on down the slope to the stream at the bottom. She takes a drink and sits beside a large rock. I watch her resting there and let my mind drift.

There will definitely be some grouse here, as there are on similar ground at home. And if Nigel wants this to be for partridge, as I think he does, he will not need any trees because partridge, unlike pheasants, are birds of the open country. I can see how birds will fly from both sides over the valley and where I will need to be to do my job of finding and retrieving them. In just a few moments, I have planned how the season would work.

I move a little and sit on some soft-looking heather. Kate moves from her large rock and starts her way back up the hill towards me when, suddenly, she stops and holds her nose in the air. She stands motionless for a few seconds and then rushes to her left and pushes into the nearest clump of heather. A bird springs up with a frightful noise of cackling and screaming that even stops Nigel and Billy talking, as they point after the bird.

The valley is below, but beyond I can see for miles and realise how beautiful it is. The sun comes out, it is a delightful place, and will be on a similar day in the season. But I can see how exposed it is and, if the wind rises and the rain comes, how hard my work will be then.

I doze as we drive home, but really my mind is on this new adventure. It will mean several extra days and more parties at the castle, more exciting episodes in all weathers, but also more strain on my good nature as I tolerate more incompetent visiting dogs! However, excitement has gripped me. Kate is asleep. I look at her and wonder how she will change the way we work both this new ground and the old. When she wakes, we will talk about the ground and the birds. Perhaps she will foresee a successful season to distract her from her dark 'cloud.'

I am restored. The visit to the new place, and the challenges it gives lift my spirits. Yesterday and today have been quiet days, and I have been able to regain my energy and really think about the future. I see much that is positive. A few years ago, we held some sporting days specialising in partridge. I was a young dog, and my responsibilities would have been limited, but it was easier than pheasant days. I know that some partridge can be more challenging as they are smaller and can change direction more easily. However, being found in open country, they are easier to flush and easier to find afterwards and, because they are smaller, easier to carry. I think of more chances to be out on the moor, of meeting more people and more dogs – it will all be wonderful! But then, hovering like a cloud of my own, are Ian, Gwen and the body. They want to spoil everything that matters!

Kate appears and looks at me with a critical eye.

'You're looking especially vague today; I should have thought this new place world have really got you going.'

If there is something I hate more than a sullen Kate, it's the Kate who wants me to feel stupid.

'It has', I reply, knowing full well that Kate will have some dynamic plans for next season that she wants to explode upon me.

She clears a dead twig from her side of our rest below the cedar tree and pushes Joe's old cap to one side.

'Clearly the partridge will need to fly across the one valley the ground possesses and, as I'm sure you know, they can then be driven straight back.'

'Depending on the wind', I add promptly. I am keen to appear as knowledgeable as her.

Kate looks at me sharply. 'Yes', is all she says. She stands to watch Peter drive in front of the castle with a load of old boxes on the buggy and then continues, testing me.

'So, a good lot of partridge have flown over the valley, but the wind is blowing hard and straight into the faces of the birds we now want to fly back. What do we do?'

I see the question coming, but my mind is distracted by the old cap. I force myself back to the partridge.

'We could make them fly into the wind but place the guests down stream of it so when the birds drift, the guests are in the right place.'

I have hit the spot! Kate is instantly impressed and rushes on about placing guests in the little side glen that she noticed joins the main valley in just the right place. She has noted where she would need to be to retrieve them. As she becomes more technical, I allow my mind to relax. At last, I have said something that pleases her.

11

'Why have you brought Joe's old cap?', I ask Kate, but she is distracted and doesn't respond. I try again.

'Did you hear me say that the body was dressed in the same pattern of tweed as Joe's old cap.'

Her mind is back with me now. She looks across, surprise etched on her face.

'No. When did you realise this?'

'When Nigel gave it to you. I said as soon as I recognised it - though you may have left by then.'

She looks at me as though this is the missing part of the puzzle. I prepare for a long lecture.

'Haven't you wondered why your man was killed? A man with no connection to anyone or anything here at the castle or up the valley?'

'Yes, of course I have, and I realised there may be a link.'

Kate rounds on me with unusual anger.

'Of course, there is a link! Was your body about the same size as Joe?' She doesn't wait for an answer and rushes on. 'Your man was clearly killed by mistake by someone thinking he was Joe. Then Joe was killed after, once the mistake was realised!'

She stands, stretches and shakes herself thoroughly.

'We've spent our time worrying about how the killer attacked the man and whether he walked or drove, when we should have been concentrating on working out who wanted Joe dead.' Her anger is subsiding, and practicality is taking over.

'It has to be someone around here, someone to do with the sporting days.'

The candles on the dining table are lit; it must be an especially important dinner. Ian runs around checking everything is right, and there are so many knives, forks, and glasses on the table I worry there won't be room for the food. I have hidden myself safely under the table, from where I watch the team rush here and there, but my mind is still on the cap.

It was Joe's, and has been given to Kate as a memento, something to smell him by. Is that relevant or just an amazing coincidence? Kate doesn't believe in coincidence. She is sure the cap gives her the answer - but then perhaps it's too simple. Others wear that pattern of tweed; is she seeing what someone wants her to see? Or maybe it's what she wants to see.

I am a healthy dog. I have strong legs and paws, bright eyes and a fine shiny coat. However, as with many Spaniels, I do suffer with my ears. What has been a bearable itch has become an inflamed pain and I must see the vet. I have heard it said, especially by Labradors and Retrievers after a difficult day in the field when their courage has been severely tested, that we Spaniels deserve what we get. It is true that we do put our ears where few - and certainly few of those breeds - would put theirs. When we are working, we do so with a single purpose, and our own welfare is seldom considered. We live and work with our nose and, where our nose goes, our ears are obliged to follow.

You may well be asking, as indeed I did when I saw the problem was growing: why should I be suffering now, when the sporting season is well behind me? What could I possibly have done to bring it on? As Nigel drives me to the vet, I try to think. My last working trip up the valley was several weeks ago and my visit to the new ground did not involve any hunting. No, it could only be the lake. As you know, I frequently swim in the lake to clean myself and, recently, with the arrival of summer weather, the weed has started growing. I hope I am wrong. The idea of no more lake swimming would make the balance of my rabbit control and castle hospitality very difficult.

I don't like vets. I visit them rarely, I am glad to say, because every time they cause me pain. The surgery is large and bright and the staff are cheerful, but I still find it depressing. I'm in the waiting room and on my right is a very sick-looking terrier. She has an old leather lead and is lying at her mistress's feet. She doesn't look at me and when she's called needs to be picked up and carried like a bundle of washing. On my left is a plastic box with a mesh lid and a very frightened black cat peering out. We sit, waiting like wet dogs on a wet day. The rest of the sickly gathering are house pets on pretty leads, often wearing awful coats, or sad cats with sad-looking owners.

Eventually it's our turn and we walk to a side room. I am asked to stand on a table, and they take my temperature, then put liquid in my ears. Nigel is given some cream and a packet of tablets, but there is no mention of the lake, so I keep those thoughts to myself. Thankfully, I seem to have escaped relatively unscathed this time.

🐾

I haven't seen Gwen recently and Nigel has been carrying on as if nothing bothers him, which has me a little worried. I try to stay with him most of the time, to keep him safe and away from Gwen, and today we have come to the loch, a place that doesn't interest Gwen at all, so I am fairly relaxed.

Already two fishermen are out in their boat, and there may be more because I can't see behind the island. We are where the track meets the loch, beside the boathouse, and I hear the water lapping gently against the posts that support the platform where Nigel is standing. He is looking for something or someone, and I am on the shore, wondering if I can take a swim.

Why we are here? I have only been to this spot once, on a sporting day, when the wind blew strongly, and Billy thought the birds from the high wood would fly this way. They didn't, and we haven't tried it since.

Nigel jumps down from the platform and walks along the narrow path that follows the right bank of the loch. I wait till he rounds the bend and is hidden by a crab apple tree before I slide gently into the water. It is clear and cooler than I expected, much cooler than the lake by the castle, but I know the snow has only just left the moor above the high wood and that's where this water comes from, tumbling over a waterfall and through an old oak wood.

I want there to be duck on the loch. I love it when the duck fly in, especially as the sun sets, giving me a chance to work and swim at the same time. For a while I just float and let the feeling soak through my whole body. I drift to the shore, where the crab apple roots have been exposed by the lapping water, and immediately I scent a rabbit. I race uphill, behind the large rocks and across an area of loose shale that rattles down the hill as I run. The scent grows, I round another boulder and dive into a patch of ferns there. The rabbit scuttles away downhill just as a pheasant springs up and climbs, noisily, high over the loch. The sight and sound of it brings a loud call from Nigel, and I scamper back to the loch. He is no longer alone; Sarah has brought a picnic!

We stay there for a long time, and I learn a great deal. I hear them say that Tim is not improving, and that Oliver is going away too. I expect them to talk about the sporting days and the lunches that Sarah does, and perhaps about Gwen too, but they say none of this. A chill starts to creep over the loch as we head home, though the faces of Nigel and Sarah look red and warm enough!

Kate has snuggled under the cedar tree.

'Gwen was talking to Ian as I came out', she says, clearly wanting me to interrupt. I resist, and she continues.

'She had just returned from somewhere and was carrying some papers with pictures of old jewellery. They were studying them, and I only managed a quick glance, but one looked very much like the ring we found under the stones.'

I look up! Could Gwen have found something from our haul?

'So, they want Gwen to marry Nigel, and they are looking for treasure. Why? Are those things linked? It's time we started to see more of what they are up to!'

Kate doesn't reply but groans and looks away. She knows I'm right.

The castle is busy. Susan and Diana, the housekeepers, blitz the main sitting room next to the big dining room and, upstairs, the small dining room is set for a dinner party. I am used to this before a weekend, when a wedding fills the marquee and the lawns echo with the shrill sounds of children, but the marquee is empty; I have checked! No one has time to talk. Nigel is tying up the rose by the front door, so I wander over to him and lie down.

Some dogs might be put out by all this action, none of which involves them. They might feel ignored, even unwanted. However, I've learnt that when the team are all pulling towards an important deadline, as we undoubtedly are today, it doesn't matter whether I am a key part of the team or not, I need to either muck in or keep my head down. Nigel is still busy; he trims a part of the rose that has died and ties up the rest. I clear the debris and carry the branch away, ignoring the thorns that prick against my mouth.

Nigel admires his handy work. If he has time to gloat, he has time to tell me what's happening. He strokes my back, smiles, turns and walks indoors. I follow, but when he goes into the kitchen, I go upstairs, taking them in several springing strides. Candles are on the table and the smell of recently baked cake drifts from downstairs. I smile to myself in the full-length mirror. I can see what's happening; an important birthday dinner is to be held upstairs. A dinner with cake, and probably beef too.

🐾

Gwen is talking to Sarah over the garden fence. Sarah is young, though not as young as Gwen, and with a face showing more age than it should. They are discussing Tim and when they look at me I feel uncomfortable and start to move away. Sarah calls and points towards the door. Yes! She is inviting me to go in, and I am through the fence as if invited to chase a rabbit. I want to know if Tim is as improved as he hoped to be - as I want him to be. I have so much to tell him.

His eyes turn to me a little as I go in and I sit by his feet, so he can see me easily. I tell him about my ears, then start on the new shoot and the grouse that made such a noise. I look into his eyes and realise he is happy. It doesn't matter what I talk about, he just loves to hear me and reply through his eyes. It's my excitement he loves as much as my thoughts. I stay longer today because his eyes don't close, and I think he is getting better. I will come every day he wants me and try to tell him a good story every time.

The guests for the dinner arrive in the early evening, looking very smart. The dinner is special, with the best fillet steak and the finest wines. Ian is happy when he serves such a meal, and Gwen loves to float about looking important. I play no part but am happy too. I am confident the party will not be big eaters and there'll be a good helping left for me. However, they are slow eaters, and compound this by making speeches.

I walk outside to escape and look at the water. I have not swum since my visit to the vet, except for my dip in the clear, cool waters of the loch, and I've missed it. I think of taking a dip but make do with looking into the breeze and sniffing the weather. I sense someone behind me and turn to see Kate. She glances at me and then looks across the water.

'No rain tonight', she says, 'and how are our rabbits?' Though she has asked a question, she moves away without waiting for my answer.

A warm feeling flows through me. It has nothing to do with rain or rabbits but is because she has said 'our' rabbits. Perhaps whatever barrier there has been between us is going. Can we be a team at last? I walk across the lawn and go back into the castle, where Kate is waiting on the sofa.

'Well, and how do I deserve this honour?' I say, with a confidence I expect to be destroyed by some cutting reply.

'I think I owe you an apology and an explanation', she replies.

For a moment, I think she's waiting for me, but she's just looking for the right message and after a few seconds she goes on. 'I should have helped you more and thought less.'

Then she is silent again, for longer this time, and I know she's finding it difficult to explain her thoughts.

'I've been too busy trying to work out my senses. I should have been with you doing everyday things and left them to sort themselves!'

'Well, you can start now by helping me check the lake', I say, jumping down from my seat. 'There is something on this afternoon and I don't know what it can be, but whatever it is, we had best be ready.'

The checking takes only a few minutes, and we return to the cedar tree.

'I know you don't believe Joe's death was an accident. Is that why the 'cloud' won't leave you alone?' I have wanted to say these words for a while.

'Yes, I didn't think it was and now I'm sure. We were run off the road, and I was thrown forward and knocked out. Joe was found outside the car. He had a blow to his head that was fatal, and no other vehicle remained at the scene.'

She has said it before, but the logic of her words now strikes me.

'And you think the body in the flood was meant to be Joe? Someone made a terrible mistake, and they followed this up by causing the crash?'

Kate looks at me with a nod.

'When I realised the two men were wearing the same tweed, my suspicion became certainty. The murderer must be someone who wanted to silence Joe and who was either present at, or knew about the day when the first death occurred. It was someone who knew Joe's tweed and was able to go down to the meadow without attracting suspicion.'

She stops and scratches an ear, before continuing.

'But it's not as simple as that, is it? If they were closely involved, they wouldn't have mistaken the guest for Joe just because the tweed was the same. I think it must have been someone that was told to kill a man in that particular tweed, but they didn't know Joe himself.'

It's now my turn to nod. 'Or the date - remember he was killed several days before Joe was due here.'

We both look at each other.

I think about the team that persuade the birds to fly, those who help me find those that are down, the picker's up, perhaps even a guest. All people I thought I could trust! But all this seems dwarfed by the fact that someone desperately wanted to kill Joe. I struggle to accept this, to believe that anyone would want to harm him!

🐾

A lorry arrives in mid-afternoon, followed by several old cars carrying a gaggle of young people. They empty the lorry and start building on the lawn. I move from my cedar tree and Nigel reassures me; he says it's a stage, whatever that is! At first, I try to help, but then just stand back and watch. Kate is bewildered too and returns to the cedar tree.

By late afternoon everything is ready, and the young people are resting, eating or sorting their costumes. Is it going to be another dinner? Are they going to pretend to be someone they are not? Is there going to be another pretend murder? A barbeque will offer hot dogs (a tasteless name for very tasty food!) and a bar selling drinks has been set up under the trees. A few groups arrive, keen to find a good spot on the lawn, and I introduce myself. This done, I walk up the lawn and into the trees at the top.

It's still daylight and will be for a while yet. I want to see how it all looks now and picture how it will look with both the usual lights that illuminate the castle and the extra ones being put up on the stage. Kate joins me; has she worked out what is going to happen? I look at her, but she just shrugs her shoulders and scratches an ear. There will be no lighting on the lawn, and this is important, as it means more food may be dropped or knocked over!

I look at the audience as they arrive and notice where they set their folding chairs and picnic tables. I must plan my time to maximise the benefits. I pick up the aroma of sausages cooking. The barbeque has started, and I wander over. Steve the second chef, is busy; a crowd is gathering, and Kate is already there.

Night falls and the team in their fine dresses and amazing outfits are in full swing. I try to understand it but fail. I believe it is something by someone called Shakespeare, but I am none the wiser, and Kate still looks utterly bewildered. I am disappointed and pleased in equal measure. At last, I can handle something she can't! As I look at the actors, and the way they pretend to be someone they are not, I try to imagine Joe's killer. No one stands out.

I'm on my second tour of the lawn. Most guests are in crooked rows near the stage, and others are in groups across the lawn. Three old ladies sit near the lake, and I'm glad Nigel switched off the fountain or they wouldn't hear a thing. I sit by them for a while and receive a stroke and a sausage for my efforts. Only one party has children, and they are right in the middle, enjoying a picnic. The children are so quiet I almost miss them. I sit on their blanket and enjoy their affection, but am not offered anything, not even a bone. I move back by the barbeque, where the smell is reassuring, and the view is good. Suddenly the lights grow, the audience stands, and everyone claps. It must be over, and I stand too.

I think of Tim; he would have enjoyed tonight. I must make sure I remember all the important details to tell him tomorrow. Everyone packs their chairs and tables and looks for somewhere to put the food they haven't eaten, and I offer to clear it for them. Why do people eat so many salads? I will never like them. I am quite full now; sausages, chicken and cold beef pies; food I don't recognise but which tastes good; and sandwiches. The actors clear up, all the guests seem to be leaving happy and I give them my customary farewell.

I do a final tour of the grounds. The moon has disappeared behind clouds and a chill breeze suddenly grows. I am beside the lake, near the spot where Steve cooked his hot dogs. A feeling draws me towards the summerhouse; it grows stronger and the chill creeps through my body.

At first, I see nothing. Most of the lights have been turned off and the darkness seems intense, but then the moon forces its way out again. Does it want to tell me something? A sense of evil fills me, and I close my eyes. I don't want to open them but must! When I do, I see Jane slumped in the corner. She could have been sleeping, were it not for the large blood stain across her chest.

12

The police appear, the lawn is out of bounds, and lights are everywhere. The tape they put around the lake reminds me of my body and makes me shake. Why am I always the first to find them?

Kate has no answer. She can see so much when it doesn't matter, but when I need her, she just says it doesn't add up.

'Let me sleep on it', she says. What help is that?

The night passes as it did the night of that first body, over again. I see the darkness slowly becoming dawn and want it all to have been a bad dream but know it's not! The sounds of morning come before any of us are ready, and an army of police search the lawns and the ground behind the lake. I offer to help - after all, I know the area better than anyone - but am turned away.

Ian has been driven off in a police car. They say he turned up at the castle at about the time I found Jane's body. He was dumb with shock and his shirt was soaked with blood. I try to picture Ian as a killer, and I really want to, but can't. Is it because I hate Ian so much or that I loved Jane? What is happening to my world?

The more I am kept from walking on the lawn, the more I want to go there. Jackdaws caw in the lime trees and cars drive slowly past. They all have questions, so many questions.

Tim is in his garden, which is a good sign, and Kate is with him. I join them. He heard much of the performance through his bedroom window, which makes my job much easier. He doesn't know about Jane's death. He must have been asleep and, as we know so little anyway, we don't tell him. He will find out soon enough.

Tables fill the lawn, and policemen and policewomen sit at each one, talking to the guests from last night's audience, who have been asked to return. Nigel has laid on free drinks, coffee and lemonade. I wander slowly around, sitting a while under each table. Everyone is stunned or bored, with little in between. They say they saw Jane during the evening - helpful, kind, smiling - but believe they had left before anything happened. I think of Jane, hear her kind and gentle voice that will be no more and am overwhelmed with sadness.

So, no one saw anything. I carry on beyond the summerhouse and duck, unnoticed, under the awful tape. It is surprisingly quiet here. I check I am alone and slip down into my tree camp. Yes, it is still where I put it in my haste last night: the sheet of paper Jane had clasped in her hand! I push it into the corner where the sparkling bracelet lives and continue my journey.

You may ask why I don't give the paper to Nigel, or straight to the police. Well, I have seen enough of their ways and lengths of tape, and I don't trust them to find the answers that I know will come to Kate and me, eventually.

The paddock beyond the garden compound is full of wildflowers and thick clumps of nettles. Many have been flattened by yesterday's search - the one they wouldn't let me help with. I follow the fence. If someone came this way, they would have to climb it somewhere. I reach the bottom, where the fence meets the road to the cottage, and I find it. Weak, very weak, but definite. Someone climbed the fence here; the wooden rails have held the scent. Would a policeman have done it? No, I decide, so who? I sniff again, but no name comes.

Nigel is running around, and with wedding guests due any moment, I can see why. When can we use the lawn? Where can people go? Can we even hold the wedding? All these must be answered, and soon!

Kate and I go to the cottage. She wants to talk about her 'cloud', and I want to hear.

'My cloud has settled, though I don't know why.'

I can think of an obvious answer and can't resist saying it,

'Perhaps it was for Jane, not Tim, and now she's gone, it has too.'

'No, although I can see it may look that way. No, I didn't see it yesterday either, nothing had changed. If it had been for Jane, it would have become very intense, and it didn't.'

'So why didn't you see Jane's death? I don't understand, how do your 'clouds' select their target?'

Kate has no answer for me, and just shrugs her shoulder. Then she looks up.

'Perhaps it only appears around people who matter to us.'

I am unimpressed. Jane was important to me, very important. She really mattered! I hope my look says this.

Kate is surprised by my reaction but just shakes her head.

'I am sure something is going to happen; I just don't know what and when. Sometimes, just as I think the cloud has passed, I wake in the night. It's as if someone is knocking with a very important message, but when I answer, no one is there.

'But you saw Gwen and Ian before, what of them?' I ask before she can move away. 'You saw them cornering Nigel why didn't you see Jane's death?' I wait for her answer!

She looks at me wanting understanding. I want to be angry with her for not having the answer I want but can tell she is suffering too. I see tears in her eyes and my anger subsides. I want to help her, to show my love for her, and I hope my look achieves it. I am still annoyed, annoyed that Jane's impending death didn't warrant a cloud, but before we can continue, the door bursts open and two young boys run through. The wedding guests are arriving!

Ian is back, though he and Gwen are in a poor way. Both are suffering from shock. I look into their eyes, but can only find a vague, distant look. Something says their shock is genuine, but as it sits among so many lies, I can't be sure. Gwen was with guests in the castle; she has eight people who can back her up. However, Ian is another matter. He says he heard a shout as he tidied the barbeque after the play. He ran to the summerhouse to see a figure running away and Jane standing, but bleeding badly. He held her in his arms, but soon realised she had died, and sat her in the corner. Is this true? I can't be sure.

🐾

Nigel has taken us to the rearing field. The wedding happened, though few were able to smile and most left as soon as they could. We need to escape the castle and the sadness that lingers there. Nigel is pretending to be interested in the birds and I am beside him, trying to sleep. Kate walks over to us.

'It's the cloud', she whispers. She looks over to where Nigel is standing. 'It's hovering over him.'

Her face is full of fear. She thinks it involves him, that it's meant for him. We are both shocked. I hoped her cloud had settled and that its settling meant her worries over Tim were exaggerated. Now, it seems to be spreading like a winter's fog.

Kate takes to her bed and only appears when she thinks no one is about. I am worried and frustrated. Jane's death makes no sense, so much goodness amongst the wickedness. She must have discovered something that was very important; very important indeed!

All we have gained in the last few days seems threatened. In a strange way, Jane's death has rekindled my need to solve the mystery of my man's body. I had hoped to use our time up the valley to have a good look at where I found the body. I missed the cartridge bag and feel there is something else I missed!

Nigel is also affected. He goes quietly to do Oliver's work or sits silently in the office; but whatever I do, he ignores me. If the 'cloud' is for him, how will it affect him? Is this moodiness an effect of the cloud too, or the Gwen effect? Is it Jane's death, or is the timing a coincidence? I want to think it is just about Jane's death, so close to home and so brutal. I looked at Ian this morning. Gwen has gone away, but he hasn't - perhaps the police won't let him? I want to know how he really feels. He is returning to his shell, where he hides his wickedness. It's time I shook him out of it!

I make my way to my camp below the scraggy pine tree. The police have gone now, and all that remains is the mud around the summer house where they trampled, and a short length of tape fluttering from a post. I slide down into my hide away and look at the sheet of paper that Jane carried. Did the killer know she had it? Will they be looking for it? I wish Kate could escape from her 'cloud', we need two minds working, not one!

I look at the bracelet, and it sparkles back. The rest of the horde will be safe where they are, this will be bait enough! I carry it to the summer house, along with a fragment of Jane's paper, a piece that was attached to the main sheet.

Now the police have finished their tests and left, someone has tried to clean up. A strong smell burns my nose, but a dull stain still shows where Jane lay. I look at the stain for a moment, trying to replace it with the warmth of Jane's memory. It makes me more determined to find her killer. I place the bracelet on the paper in the corner, weighing it down, and both will hopefully excite and confuse the man who finds them.

I look around, back towards the marquee, across towards Tim's garden, towards the lake and the road beyond, but no one is about, so I wander slowly to the cedar tree and wait. Ian always goes to the summer house before lunch. There he can smoke happily and sometimes meet Gwen. Will he change his routine today, when so much has happened and Gwen is away? I don't think so and I will see him clearly from my hide away.

Ian is late, but there is no mistaking the slight shuffle as he exits the main door, looks about and heads for the summer house. I fear he will miss my bait; he is obviously looking forward to his cigarette, but then enough sparkle catches his eye to draw him to it. I have moved across the lawn and am lying idly by the lake, but with a good view into the summer house. He doesn't notice me; his mind has been captured! He drops onto one knee and lifts the bracelet and fragment of paper from the spot on the floor where I have left them. I watch him lift them. Is he surprised? I'm sure he is, but he is looking away and I can't see his eyes. Then he turns and faces me. I have never seen a face like it, such shock!

I feel myself smiling. 'You always were a greedy man, which will matter most, the paper or the jewel?'

He brandishes the jewel, holding it in front of him to catch the light, then slides it into his pocket and looks at the paper.

'So, I was right', I beam.

I know he will soon tell Gwen what he has found. Their impatience will reveal them, and Kate and I will be ready.

We are about to host our third wedding in three days, and no one has the energy to be grumpy or to dream. Everyone is still in shock, and without Jane's calming ways, everything is much more difficult. Kate offers to help today so I stand back and leave her to it. There are fewer guests, about half the number from yesterday and the day before, and they are a dull lot. I'm happy they are dull, I'm so tired.

I'm resting in the small office behind reception, hoping no one will find me. Everything seems to be going well and if Kate has any problems, she hasn't troubled me with them. I set to washing myself. With all the excitement of the last few days I have let this slip. I push my leg behind my ear and a jab of pain runs through me. I felt it earlier when I followed the scent line down the paddock fence. I hope it goes soon; I don't have time for distractions.

I have told Kate what I did with the bracelet and the piece of paper, and she was not amused. She thinks she has enough stress from the 'cloud', without encouraging more. However, she can see that what I did might work, and I have promised to be on hand whenever she needs me. Someone opens the door to the marquee and the music starts. The meal must be over, so I drag myself around to the kitchen. I wait patiently, hoping my efforts of the last three days will be rewarded with some of the roast beef that I smell waiting in the kitchen. Kate joins me and shares our little feast; she deserves it!

13

Today I nearly died? How could this happen to a dog as fit and active as me? It only took a second when my thoughts were elsewhere and my concentration away.

Some guests arrived; it was a lovely evening for a walk and I decided to go with them.

We turned right out of the gates and my nose became full of the scent of rabbits. Both sides offer thick undergrowth with bushes, willow herb and young trees, and soon I was hunting. They ran in all directions, and I chased a couple into the field above the road. As I returned, one leapt up under my feet. I was on him in a second and about to catch him when he turned onto the road. I followed without thinking, straight into the path of a car!

I'm told I went right under it, and no one could see how I could have survived.

Everyone was distraught, and more because the car driver didn't seem to care at all! Talk of insurance and blame were swept away as the guests made him drive me back to the castle, from where a very shocked Nigel took me to the vet, while Kate waited with a look no one had ever seen before.

The vet examined me, while the future of the estate hung in the balance, and the car that hit me sits in the castle drive. The driver claimed I caused such damage that it's unsafe for him to continue and, contacted neighbours in the hope they would agree that I am dangerous.

(As I look back, I find this funny. I am on very good terms with all our human neighbours but, had he been able to ask any of the rabbits or pheasants that live in the area, he may have received the answer he wanted.)

Finally, the police were called, and the car was carted away.

Although all this may be of interest to you, I'm sure you are more concerned about my health. Good news! The vet examined and x-rayed me and found no broken bones. In the morning, as I was no worse, he allowed me home.

Naturally, I am very sore but pleased that the party the rabbits will certainly have planned to celebrate my death will now have to be cancelled. Everyone is amazed by my recovery, and I put it down to my natural strength and a lot of luck.

I look for a comfortable position. My basket seems too small, and I think of moving to the rug in the sitting room when Kate speaks.

'I should have seen it. I should have saved you, but I didn't. What sort of friend am I?'

'You did see it', I blurt out, trying to face her but only succeeding in giving myself a stab of pain.

'You saw Nigel and me at the rearing field with the 'cloud' over us, but you assumed it was for Nigel, when it was really meant for me.'

She grunts, as though my comments do not excuse her.

'And was it deliberate, did they set out to kill you?'

I laugh but regret it; the bruising is coming out.

'No, of course they didn't, no one could have known I would chase a rabbit at that very moment.'

Kate is still unsure. 'I don't believe in accidents anymore, or coincidence, and nor should you!'

I have been told to rest for several days after this brush with death. It's easy to take so much for granted and it's only now that I see what's at stake. How would the team at the castle manage without me? I carry out my duties quietly and modestly. Nigel arranges for people to bring their dogs to help pick up game but, without me, they would need many more during the season.

I know, by the love everyone shows me, that I am valued for myself too. But I have never been happy to be thought of as just a dog that children stroke and play with, and that old people admire. I am a dog with a mission. And this accident is certainly not making me more careful, or less determined to master the rabbits in the gardens, the game up the valley - or find the murderer, whoever they are!

I want to talk to Kate, but she seems wrapped up in her thoughts. However, boredom drives me to break the silence.

'I'm making a fast recovery - so fast it hardly warranted a 'cloud."

Kate seems to ignore my words, but then she walks over and sits by me.

'Yes, you were right, the cloud in the rearing field was certainly meant for you, not Nigel, and it means my ability to foresee disasters is still with me. It also means the cloud I saw those weeks ago is still hovering; it just hasn't told me where and when it will land.'

I visit Tim. I want to go the moment I am back from the vet, because I am sure he will have heard about my accident and be distressed, but I have been forcibly shut in the cottage and made to rest. When I do escape, and stand at Tim's door, I feel nervous. After all, I am not as ill as he is, and my full recovery has been predicted. No, I'm able to talk with Tim as no one else can and what would he have done if I had been killed?

He is not as well as he was, and I blame myself. I spend the whole day with him. We have little to say and just sit and look at each other, while Sarah is in the background, never far away. I lie by Tim's big window and watch him sleep.

I am nearly asleep too. As I doze, I know everyone is watching and thinking about me and, as they do so, they are less conscious of themselves.

🐾

I am banned from my sofa; they say I mustn't jump. I creep through to the small office and curl up under the desk. The reception was unmanned when I arrived, but now I hear Gwen's voice, and when Ian joins her, my ears prick up. A shadow appears in the doorway, checking that the small office is empty, but I am well-hidden below the desk. Satisfied, their conversation takes on a new dimension. I start to shake with excitement, waiting for them to discuss the bracelet and the note. I don't have to wait long.

'Well, what did the museum say, is it part of a haul?' Ian asks impatiently. Gwen is silent for a while, and I wish I could see her face, her eyes, but then she speaks, and I know she's smiling.

'Yes, it's Viking, and from the sixth century. The same period as the ring you found. They wanted to know where I had found it, and what else there might be.'

Silence takes over, then Ian speaks.

'So, what did you tell them?'

Gwen answers nervously, as though she is expecting to be told off.

'I said a friend had found it but I didn't know where. They accepted this for now but want the information soon.'

Again, Ian is quiet for a while; I can smell them thinking. This has been important to them but, I sense, not as important as what is to come.

'OK, that's all very interesting, but who put it there and who found the note? And how much do they know?'

Gwen becomes more assertive,

'Why didn't you take the note before you ran indoors; what were you thinking?'

Ian doesn't need telling. He is holding his head in his hands and weeping. 'I know, but it all happened so fast. He ran away leaving me holding her. I will never forget the look on her face.'

Why doesn't he say her name? Jane, her name was Jane, and she was a finer person that you could ever be! I am panting with anger. Will they hear me? No, I decide, they are too worried about themselves. They have given me part of an answer, but I need more: Jane's killer was a man, but who?

I have become unbearably stiff. I need to stretch out, but the side of the desk prevents me. I make myself wait, and I'm glad I do. As Ian leaves, the phone rings and Gwen answers. She's back on charm offensive and Jane is just a memory. At last, she finishes and moves upstairs – finally, I can leave!

I meet Kate coming from the cottage and we walk together to the cedar tree.

'Well, what did they say?', she demands.

Surely, she knows? But, before I can answer, Nigel appears and calls us. He says that Billy's assistant is leaving, and a new boy has come for an interview and to look at the estate. Kate jumps into the Land Rover, but I am told to wait and am lifted carefully onto the seat, as a basket of eggs just collected from the hens.

The interview apart, it is good to see the valley again especially as some of the birds are now released into the woods and are growing their adult feathers. Nigel hops in beside me and we drive along the road that looks down on the river.

The body shouts to me and I want to look away, but a stronger urge keeps telling me to go there. I am sure all the tragedies this summer stem from it and must find a way of putting them together.

Already, the once-bare thorn bushes are bright and green, and the sheep look different without their wool. Billy wants to show something to Nigel, so they pull over and walk up the field. Andy, the new boy, follows.

Nigel often stops here, just as he did when I first saw the body, when snow carpeted the ground, and the valley was full of water and ice. The door has been left ajar, and, again, Kate is asleep. I look at her, smile, nose open the door and slide carefully to the ground. The landing hurts, but I ignore it and head for the valley. The grass is growing well, as are the thistles and dandelions, especially by the hedge that leads to the bottom land. The rushes are tall and thick, much thicker than when I found the body, but I know where it was; I can never forget.

I look down the valley to where Kate found the cartridge bag; why should it have been down there? It was Hamish's bag, but what did it have to do with the body? I wish Ben had seen it; he would know. I hear voices calling loudly - Billy and Nigel are looking for me. I turn to obey but, as I do, my nose brushes against a string. No, it's not a string, it's an old boot lace, and attached to it is a whistle! It has snagged on the thorn hedge. I carry it back to the vehicle, to Nigel. He wants to be angry that I left, but he's distracted by the whistle - and mystified.

Later, Nigel is in the gun room, and I am watching. I think he has forgiven me and is relieved I didn't injure myself, but mostly he is mystified by the whistle.

'You recognise it, don't you, Mutley?', he says, waving it in the air. I nod but want him to confirm it.

'It belongs on a hook in the lunch barn, it's my spare.' He smiles. 'And, as you know, I sometimes forget my number one whistle, so you see it often enough.'

Yes, that's what I thought it was, but what was it doing near the body? You haven't worked with me there for months. You know where I had been but didn't ask exactly where I had found it.

Am I doubting Nigel too now? Can I trust no one?

The gun room looks like just any room with an ordinary-looking door, but Nigel needs a special key and must type numbers into a box on the wall before he can enter. The door is heavy, the window barred, and the side wall has chains to hold guns in a rack. It is very warm. At the far end are the guns used by Nigel. Soon, guest guns will join them; standing in line, waiting for the next day on the moor or in the woods, and beside them is a large box of fireworks, ready for a wedding. I thought Nigel had cleaned this room at the end of the season, but it is dusty! A pile of empty boxes stands in the corner, with a bag of used cartridge cases and old cleaning cloths.

Sarah climbs the stairs, looks in at the mess and smiles.

'You found the old cap I dropped in', she says, peering through the dust.

Nigel looks up, his brow filthy where the dust has stuck to him.

'Yes, thank you, but I thought it came up with Joe's things.'

'No,' she replies, 'I found it on a hook in the lunch barn. I thought you might know whose it was.'

She glides down the stairs and Nigel returns to his cleaning.

No, I whisper to myself. If it didn't come with Joe's things, it was in the lunch barn to tell someone what to look for!

Nigel is now packing away some fishing gear, clearing the table that will be used for cleaning and putting everything in its place. I lie by the door; I love the smell! It is a mixture of gunpowder and gun oil, together with the unmistakable scent of once-wet clothes that have dried in a confined space. After several months without a whiff of such things I find all these scents very romantic.

That night I tell Kate about the whistle and the cap. The cap had held pride of place in her bed since she recovered from the shock that came with Nigel giving it to her, but now she has pushed it to one side, its meaning tarnished!

I wake with rabbits fresh in my mind, but when I arrive at the castle, Sarah is there. She gets up from the desk and smiles at me.

'Do you fancy a walk'?

She doesn't wait for an answer but opens the door and looks for me to follow. We go down through the farm and on to the old barn that is used for lunches on sporting days. The track weaves into the valley, starting beside Tim's house, crossing the stream by the old mill, and climbing steeply by the fields that run up to the farm buildings. In the field to the left are the hens. Chickens, not female pheasants, but when I was young, I didn't know the difference and caught two before I learnt.

Nigel wants a cover crop here, but Oliver thinks the shooting would scare the hens and stop them laying, so it is still grass. The castle is half hidden by trees and I try to peer through them, but as I do, I am suddenly giddy and nearly fall. It must be another 'cloud', one Kate will be suffering more than me. I want to be with her but know I can't without making a fuss; she will have to manage.

The lunch barn is cool and smells of paint. The long table is in the middle of the room, and the grate sits clean and cold. Nigel has been painting the walls and all the pictures of long-ago sporting days are stacked in the corner. I enjoy the cool and lie by the fireplace that warms me in the winter. I hear the comforting sound of Sarah working in the kitchen, and then she looks around the corner. She wants to make sure our walk has not been too much for me.

'You know Tim is very ill. You knew before any of us, but you are his strength. He needs you so much!'

I am too surprised to answer, and all I can do is look at her. Soon I am asleep. Whether it's the effect of the walk, or the accident, or the 'cloud', I don't know, but I'm dreaming. Nigel is very young, and so are his guests, but Billy is just the same and so am I. Billy doesn't want the boys to shoot many birds, but they want to bag as many as they can, and every drive is a contest that both want to win. I support the boys because the bigger the bag, the more I will have to retrieve and the more fun I will have! Gwen keeps appearing and disappearing, like the sun in April.

Suddenly I am awake, and Sarah is looking down at me - I'm so pleased it's not Gwen! She is looking worried. I'm breathing fast, and she thinks it's an effect of my accident, but I know it's because I have been retrieving a bird in my dream. I leap up and race outside to show her that I'm fine, and soon we are laughing and enjoying the afternoon sun. As we return to the castle, we climb the hill that's growing in front of us and I want to run to Kate, but I know Tim is waiting.

It must be difficult for him, with so many ideas inside his head and no chance to get up and run them off. Is that why he likes my tales so much - the chance to live excitement through me? Already, with the season still only a dream, I am a nervous wreck of anticipation. What will I be like when it really arrives? Sarah says Tim can come to my lawn when he is stronger. This is great news and already I'm making plans for it. I can see the effect on him too; at last, he has something good to look forward to.

I leave Sarah and Tim and walk back to the castle. Sarah has tried to appear her old self, but I know the death of Jane still haunts her and adds to her worry over Tim and Oliver. Only Kate and I know Jane's death was not the first murder, but the third. We must not be distracted by the coming season; it's time to put all the information together.

Kate is waiting for me, annoyed.

'Didn't you sense the 'cloud', didn't you know I needed you?' she demands as we walk by the lake.

'Yes, I sensed it, but I can't always drop everything. What happened, anyway?'

I try not to look apologetic. Kate looks at me and then continues.

'Gwen cornered Nigel in the little office; she told him she is pregnant!'

I'm shocked, so this is the thing she had to do.

'She's not pregnant, is she?', I ask, though I'm sure she isn't.

'No, of course she's not, but Nigel won't know that, and it may be enough in his troubled state to push him into marrying her.'

I roll over and face her.

'Whilst I was with Sarah this morning, I had a dream; one I hadn't had before. It was about Nigel as a boy, and Gwen appeared. She shouldn't have, she had no place in the dream. Was that when she was telling Nigel? Could that have been a kind of 'cloud'?

'Oh yes, that was definitely a 'cloud', and the fact that you saw it shows how important it is becoming.'

Kate looks at me as she speaks, her eyes full of worry.

The summer holidays are here, and so are the children. It should be a wonderful time with games on the lawn and the garden at its best and, in many ways, it is. I hate routines, but the busier we are, the more I seem to fit into one!

A boy wants to play a game before leaving, so I run slowly with him around the lake and back. He is behind me now and laughing so much he can hardly walk, let alone run. I wait for him, his mother by my side, and then stand and watch as they load up and drive away. I love it when the children are excited, when they haven't seen the grounds before and can't believe how big they are. The guests go, and I stand, pretending I am not exhausted. I look about and all is at peace. I want to relax, to build my strength, but inside my mind is on fire. Why Jane? Who will be next? These questions keep appearing, and they are getting louder.

This morning, before the sun gains its full strength, I lie in its rays. Kate joins me. I close my eyes to avoid the glare, enjoying its warmth on me.

'I think we are looking at the murders in the wrong way.' Kate says, out of the blue.

I had switched off my brain to enjoy the sun and it takes a while to re-engage it.

'How?', I reply, needing more time to focus.

'We have been distracted by the mistaken identity; the fact the wrong person was killed before they caught up with Joe.'

I see she is talking about my body and agree, but there's nothing new here and I wonder when she will get to the point.

'What we need to ask is who wanted to kill Joe, and why?', she says, and looks at me for support.

'Someone must have had a very good reason to go to such trouble. Why, what did he know that was such a threat to them?'

She has said this before, and she knew her master better than anyone - she must know! And how is Jane's murder involved? I try to lead the thinking.

'You must ask yourself what he had been doing - who had he been with around that time that might be relevant?'

She sighs deeply.

'Yes, you are right, but the question may not be as huge as all that. Why did they try to kill him here first? They could have tried at our home - almost anywhere would have been easier than here, on a sporting day.'

'You told me that Joe met Ian when he first came, that he looked very surprised, worried perhaps?' I look at her as I speak. Ian had always seemed guilty to me; I could happily make him my prime suspect.

'Yes, he was my first thought. But I can't think how Joe could know anything so serious about him that would lead to murder. Even if he did, surely Ian wouldn't do it on a sporting day. He knows nothing about the estate. He would have been noticed; he might even have become lost.' We look at each other and smile at the thought.

'And how does Jane fit in?', I venture.

'I put her murder along with Joe's', Kate replies. 'She clearly found out something that someone needed to keep secret.'

'And was she killed by the same person? Her murder seems so different', I add.

'Yes, that's what worries me. Your body was killed up the valley, because they thought he was Joe and that's where they felt most comfortable.' Kate gets up and walks towards the lake. The sun is hot now, too hot!

'So, was Jane about to spill the beans, and was her death planned or spontaneous?'

We are now by the summerhouse, and it's cooler. We both enter and look about. We want answers, and somehow hope to find them here. I think of the paper I found in Jane's hand and decide now is the time to share it with Kate.

'Wait here,' I shout, and rush to my camp below the tree roots. I return, panting, with the note grasped firmly in my mouth. Kate looks at it. It is crumpled, and very soggy from my energetic return. It is clearly a typed page, with a very colourful banner along the top. The banner wants to nag me! Have I seen it before? Something says I have!

'You say you found it clasped in her hand' Kate asks.

I nod agreement.

'It's strange both your bodies had something clasped in a hand. Something you wanted to keep to yourself!'

I look at her, expecting her to laugh, to smile at least, but the look she gives me is deadly serious!

14

The sun is screaming at me from a hazy sky. I'm constantly looking for that perfect balance of temperature, moving from sunshine to shade, and Kate moves with me.

Cars arrive with loud families and louder children, and I don't have the energy. Kate and I hide in our new cool spot below a leafy shrub and, thankfully, we are not disturbed.

Nigel is just finishing mowing the lawn for the second time this week. Did it really need doing again, or is he still finding any excuse to escape from Gwen? He spots me, calls me over and tells me some excellent news. Next month, on the Glorious Twelfth - the first day of the grouse season - he is taking me with him. We head off to the gun room and he begins to polish his gun for the first time this summer. I sit, and he strokes me, looks at me and I understand. The first day is not only the best day to be out on a grouse moor, but the fact that Nigel wants to take me so soon after my accident is wonderful. With just that look, he is letting me know how important I am to him.

Now Nigel is talking to Kate. I think he is telling her why he can't take her on the Twelfth – she simply needs to learn more about walking on the moors and how a grouse day there works. I hope she understands.

Nigel finishes his gun, leaves, and I rejoin Kate, who has retreated to the lake. I expect her to mention the Glorious Twelfth - to wish me luck or say she is sorry she is not coming - but she doesn't.

Ian has been playing in a cricket match with the guests, Gwen has been relaxing with massive sunglasses and a cool drink, and Kate's eyes have been on both of them. Her 'cloud' is heavy, and though she's better at handling it now, she knows it will soon explode.

'Tonight, or in the morning, but no later', she says, with the pressure showing in her eyes. The match finishes and everyone leaves the lawn. Kate watches as Gwen heads in the direction of the cottage and Ian drives off.

The morning arrives with a clear sky, except over Kate. Nigel is away decorating the lunch hall and rehanging old pictures, whilst I am trying to keep my mind on three children who have come to lunch. They are great children, and are keen to see my underground camp, which is now bigger than ever. I should be with Kate, I know, but I have convinced myself there is little I can do. When the moment she has been dreading arrives, I will sense it too.

The nearer we get to the start of the season and the more Nigel rushes around getting ready for it, the more excited I become. I have more energy than for months. I race through the back doorway into the gardens and sprint into the rhododendron bush. It's old and covers most of the fence that separates the back lawn from the garden compound and is a favourite haunt of rabbits. There are two here and they both run onto the lawn, one heading for the paddock and the other for my camp. I chase the last one and am just on him when he jinks to the side and, as I tumble clumsily into my camp, he jogs to his burrow. I sense him laughing as he goes! I look out and pick myself up. Did anyone see me fall? I hope not! I take a good, long drink from the lake and head towards the castle. It was my first real run since the accident, and I feel good. The rabbits had best watch out, a fit Mutley will soon be back!

'Have you seen Nigel', Kate demands, as she runs to meet me.

'No.' I reply, my mind still on rabbits and wounded pride.

'I'm afraid he has fallen for Gwen's deception. The cloud has broken, and, unless he has broken up with her, I fear they are engaged'.

The front door of the castle opens, and Gwen comes out. She is dressed very smartly, and Nigel follows, a blank look on his face. Kate starts to walk away from me, as low as I have ever seen her.

'They are only engaged; a lot can happen before the wedding', I call, but she walks on as if she hasn't heard me.

The next morning it's raining on my spirits as well as my head, so I go indoors and walk the corridors. If you asked me, I would say I am looking for guests who may need me, or problems I can solve, but really, I just need to be moving. Sarah is at the desk, her goodness glowing through my dark mood. There must be hope, be a way of showing Nigel what we know to be true.

The rain stops as suddenly as it started, and I picture the birds emerging from the shelter of the woods, or the grouse and partridge from the clumps of cover where they have hidden, so the sun and wind can dry them. I feel these positive thoughts develop in my mind and head out across the lawn.

Wherever Kate is, she is not at the cottage, so I use my renewed good cheer on Tim. My excitement seems to infect him, and I think he could stand up and walk. Our eyes talk and we both look forwards to the day he visits us on the lawn. I tell him that I am away with Nigel next week and that, when I am back from the moor, I will tell him all the news.

Kate appears, she is often here now. She seems able to understand him as I do and when I'm busy, it's good to know she's here. It helps her too. She can't forget her cloud, but the closer she is to him, the sooner she'll know what will happen.

Oliver has gone to hospital. I knew it was likely, but as with many things, mention of it seemed to die away after my accident. Nigel strokes me more than usual and I know it's because he's worried. Worried about him, about doing much of his work and, of course, about Gwen.

Gwen and Nigel are officially engaged. The word races around the castle and I wonder how Sarah will take it. I think of the picnics and meetings in the lunch barn. I go to the gun room. I think Nigel will be there, but the door is shut, so he has gone out. Again, nothing is as it should be!

🐾

It's Friday, but not any Friday. I've been waiting for Nigel and am afraid the engagement may spoil things. Then he rushes in, late as usual, to pick up his gun and - of course – me! I'm in heaven. I want to remember today for ever, the day Nigel and I go together for the Glorious Twelfth, the first day of the grouse season! We travel north, and thoughts of grouse replace my worries. I'm the only dog, which is bad as I'd have liked another dog to talk to as the boys chat and drink, then chat some more.

A thick-set man in a bright tweed suit pours everyone a beer and passes Nigel his glass. Suddenly it is Joe wearing the suit, and then he is lying in the flood. I look at the body, it can't be Joe, and I know it's not Joe. The tweed wants to change, flashing like a beacon. I close my eyes and open them again. The man is back as he should be, and he is speaking.

'Do you have any family to help you with the estate?'

Nigel looks up. I move a little, to see his face. When he speaks his voice has more than a touch of sadness.

'Yes, I have one brother; he manages the farm, but he's not a sportsman.'

I think of Oliver, and how sick he is, and the meaning hits home. If Oliver dies, as I'm afraid he will, and something happens to Nigel, who will take on the land, and the castle, and the sport up the valley? The efforts of Gwen and Ian stand starkly in front of me, and the consequences of the engagement are too horrible to bear. I push them to the back of my mind; they are not married yet!

It's my second time here in the Highlands and, as the house quietens for the night, my memory drifts back.

I was a young dog, barely more than a puppy, and although I had been out on a sporting day, I hadn't even seen a grouse, let alone retrieved one. I'm lucky, and in no time, I disturb a bird, which flies away faster than I have ever seen any bird fly. Nigel fires and although everyone thinks he was on target, the grouse flies on. Later, we stop, the boys have a sandwich and a beer, and I find a cool stream, drink deeply, and lie back in the heather. Someone thinks they saw where Nigel's bird landed. The place is a long way off and in thick heather, where even an older, experienced dog would find it difficult. But, as I've said, I'm very young and full of energy and think anything is possible, so I go. Nigel comes part of the way, as the others watch and finish their beers. Just as I think I've hunted every yard of the area and am about to give up, I suddenly scent it. It's different to any other scent - I just know it must be the grouse - and there it is, lying under a clump of heather. Of course, I am a hero, it is the best retrieve in all my life!

The morning of the Twelfth comes, and reality replaces my dreams. I walk out into the garden while the boys eat breakfast. I want to be well behaved and in control but, as they start to load the cars, my shaking begins. You know it, I have told you before. It sweeps over me, like a thunderstorm can cover the sky on a summer evening, and today I am buoyed by my dream of that first successful retrieve!

As the boys exit noisily from the cottage, Nigel asks me to hop into the cage that fills the back of his car, and I do. Strange though you may find it, I love this cage. It's not large, but it means a day on the moor or in the woods and, as such, it stands for fun. On the floor is an old blanket, which, later, when I am wet and exhausted, will be the finest blanket ever made.

We meet the keeper by an old stone building. It is the same keeper who saw me make that wonderful retrieve. I'm on the top of the world and can see for miles, but I'm not alone.

To help me today will be two Pointers. These dogs are much taller than me, and longer. They are close-coated, speckled brown, and walk with total confidence. At first, I think they will ignore me, but soon they relax and accept me with a friendly sniff. These are the kings of the grouse moor. This is their time and their place. I suddenly feel very nervous.

As with so many memorable days, it passes in a flash. I flush a few birds and only retrieve one. The Pointers quarter the ground effortlessly, their long legs seem to float and, when a bird is scented, they freeze till told to move – they never rush in as I do. Their retrieving is just as controlled and amazes me. Later, as Nigel drives us home, he senses my mood and reminds me that these were two outstanding dogs doing the job they do well.

'How do you think they would handle our thick, high woods or the steep banks on a very wet day? No,' he continues, 'today was their day and your days are yet to come.'

I want to revel in today; to save my memories so deeply I will never forget them, but I can't. Nigel's face interrupts them. The sadness as he talked of Oliver linked me with all the wickedness that has filled my summer.

It's late when we arrive back at the castle and I think everyone has gone to bed, but Gwen appears and wants a report. Why I do not know; she won't understand. Nigel tells her only about his friends and the moor and the bag. He doesn't mention the Pointers and I'm pleased; it would have been beyond her. They walk upstairs, and I sense a new atmosphere.

I wake to find the cottage empty! Nigel, Gwen and Kate are already at the castle and, when I shake the night from my body, I hear the sound of the mower. I join Nigel on the lawn and walk out to him. He stops to clear some debris and asks me what I thought of our day. I run in circles, barking loudly and springing on the spot.

'So, it was good then?', he says as he remounts his machine. 'Now you know how to do it we will expect miracles next week.'

Kate approaches from Tim's garden.

I rush towards her; I can't stop myself. 'How can we prevent the wedding?'

She seems surprised by my directness.

'First, we must look at all their options, see what we are up against.' Kate hesitates, and I am too excited by yesterday to wait, so I prompt her;

'And then?'

'And then we face the hard bit. How do we show Nigel what Gwen and Ian truly are?' She gives a smile as she speaks and this cheers me; at last, she can see all is not lost.

🐾

The next two days are much busier than I had expected. Often, as I've shown you, a cricket match will mean little to me, and then only when the ball is in the lake; but today our team is playing the local town, and everything is different. The match is the same, in that the rules are the usual harsh affair that don't appreciate the input of dogs, but the opposition is another matter. The team comes with at least three children belonging to each player, resulting in an army that treats my lawn as a battlefield.

Now, as you know, I have a basic love of children and can bring the best out of even the most nervous, but an army such as this is something new. I want to entertain them, to play ball and to run around the wild areas but, just as I've regained some control, a group will disappear behind the lake, and I must run after them to make sure all is well. Afterwards, I lie exhausted, and I know there is more to come!

This is mad Monday. We have a wedding. It's not large, just thirty or so, but I have been asked to be a 'page boy'. I know the bride and some of the children, and that they love me, but I have never been a page boy and am not sure what lies ahead. I have asked Nigel what it means, but he has been very vague, which worries me. I must have a bath (apparently, a swim in the lake doesn't count) and wear a large pink ribbon around my neck. Both are bad.

I am, after all, a macho hunting dog, renowned amongst the sporting dogs as being one of the best swimmers, most fearless retrievers and hardest working dogs around. The idea of this part of my character wearing such a ribbon is absurd. The only good point is that none of my sporting friends will be at the wedding and, speaking as the actor in me, I have clearly played the part of 'wedding host' well to be considered for something so at odds with my natural character.

I am being dried with a hair drier whilst standing on a big towel, with a bridesmaid hovering, holding the wretched ribbon. A man with a camera comes in and I am shocked. Suddenly, I realise that photos will be taken at the wedding. I must make sure that if any are taken of me, they will not be shown on any sporting day. I remember when a big, fat, basset hound - the pride and joy of a bride - was to be a 'bridesmaid'. At the last minute, she hid under a car and delayed the service by half an hour. I think what a good idea that was and look for a suitable vehicle, but someone has put a lead on me, and the rest of the day is, fortunately, a blur.

What a weekend! I lie on the sofa and gradually regain my mind. Earlier, several rabbits had grazed on the lawn as though I wasn't there and last night one was even seen looking in the bar window. They have no shame!

I am being distracted. Dreaming about rabbits won't solve the Gwen problem and I force myself to focus. I have so many thoughts that don't seem linked; individual thoughts that feel important in themselves, but I don't know how they fit together.

I have joined Nigel in the gun room and my eyes keep drifting to the rack, and all the guns lined up there, but I don't know why. I am drawn to one particular gun with a very unusual patch on the butt. It is dark leather, the colour of mahogany.

Does it belong to Nigel? I can't remember him using it. I try to picture a day with Nigel holding it, but my image of him fades the more I look and is replaced by the man who became the body. Could it have belonged to him? Could it have been the gun the police were looking for? More importantly, is it the gun I saw Gwen unloading from the car and, if so, why is it hidden among the others?

🐾

On Thursday morning, Tim is sitting in his house. He listens to my story, but his eyes have dulled again. I want to ask if he will be able to come over and visit the lawn, so I can show him my tree camp, although I am scared of the answer. I think he is too ill, but Sarah appears and suggests next week, if the weather is good, and we all pretend everything is fine. I walk slowly back to the castle and see Ian coming from the direction of my camp by the scraggy tree. At first, I take no notice, but then wonder if he has been looking for more of the old jewellery. I walk slowly there, as if I'm just taking a gentle walk, hop down below the old pine and scratch with a paw. The ring shines reassuringly, so I cover it up again and come away.

Thoughts of next week become frightening, and my leg hurts in sympathy. My first time in charge of a grouse day and Tim's visit to the lawn are scary prospects.

Kate takes me to one side and lies down.

'You know Tim is growing even weaker'. She looks me in the eye, defying me to disagree. I want to, I really want to, but I know she's right.

'You are right to invite him to the lawn. I know you want to show him all the changes you have made to your tree camp, and he will enjoy it, but don't expect too much.'

The police have returned and are talking with Nigel. They are in his office, so it must be important - and secret! They don't stay long and leave without speaking to me, even though I am right by their car when they go. Nigel comes out and tells me they believe Jane's husband killed her. He shakes his head sadly and returns indoors. Should I have told him about the paper in Jane's hand? No, I decide, they've had their chance and when we show them who is really guilty, all will be made clear!

🐾

That night a group arrives with cars and trailers and the smell of sheep. Gunner would have been in his element, and so am I when I meet Harry. Harry is a big, hairy Lurcher, a sort of crossbred greyhound. I haven't met one before, but I know their speciality; to chase and catch rabbits! The sheep matter to Nigel, and would have to Gunner, because they are the same breed of sheep that used to be kept here. Yet this means nothing to me, and all I can think of is how to get Harry to help me with the rabbits. I want to tell Kate of my plans, but

I'm not sure how she will take it. Will she be excited by the prospect, as I am, or is she too occupied with her 'cloud'?

I speak up and, at first, don't think she hears me. Should I say it again? Suddenly, she leaps up, as if the message has just got to her, and she does it with so much energy that I'm knocked back.

'Where is he, when do we start?', she barks.

'Now! Come on!', I reply, glad that she's so enthusiastic, and we run to find Harry.

The three of us have great fun, and I know the rabbits won't want to venture onto my lawn again without fearing for their lives. There will be no more peering through the bar windows.

Nigel wanders over to Tim's house and I follow. Tim is asleep, and Nigel and Sarah are talking quietly in the kitchen. It is one of those balmy summer evenings that make me want to lie outside all night, so I am on Tim's patio, listening to the wasps buzzing in the apple trees and watching the bats swooping low over the garden from their home high in the castle roof. At last, Nigel appears and is surprised that I am waiting for him. It's late, but the moon is bright, and I picture the grouse enjoying the air of the open moor. My mind is on our first grouse day, but then the approach of Nigel's wedding and the need to find a solution interrupts. I hardly sleep.

It has finally arrived; the day I've been dreading and looking forward to, in equal measure. Sean and his party of four Irishmen have come for two days at our grouse.

'You lead the way, boss', Kate says with a sarcastic smile, 'and I'll follow'. All this is very unhelpful.

As the men talk and laugh, I look about me. I hear them walking towards me and know Nigel will soon call my name and we will move off. I will be taken to the world I love and know and must fight to keep it that way!

We take the land upstream and have two Pointers with us today, who help me relax. I stop on a small knoll to let a guest catch up and look into the valley. It is steep and rough, and I am working that part with Kate, leaving the Pointers to do the level top land.

In the afternoon, we bring the other side of the valley back, but the strengthened wind helps the birds escape, flying low across the sloping ground. Near the end, with the vehicles in sight, a single grouse flies from the top of the line in a long curve that takes it towards the shelter of the valley. Every man shoots at it, but only John, the man nearest me, is on target and I watch as the bird locks its wings, glides past and into the heather around the corner. As retrieves go, it is easy, but as I turn the corner and take my bird to Nigel, I now know I am fit and can face the season. Kate gives me a congratulatory look and a covey of partridges springs up and goes with the wind, reminding me that the first partridge day is near.

The next day we go to the high hill. There are no Pointers, so I am the main dog and am thrilled that as we drive home at the end of the day, the guests are laughing and seem so happy.

In the morning, John is last to leave at ten, still thanking me for his first grouse. As his car trundles down the driveway, I run over to Tim's. Will he be in his garden, or at least in the sitting room? There's no sign of him. Then Sarah appears and leads me through to Tim's bedroom, where he is sleeping peacefully. I feel at any moment he will open his eyes, and I will give him my news, but he just sleeps. I lay down near his bed, where he will see me right away, if he wakes, and stay there until Nigel looks round the door and signals me to follow him.

I know that Nigel and Sarah should be together, holding hands, and that they both want to. Before the engagement announcement they would have – Kate and I must put a stop to Gwen's plans!

It's another morning, where did yesterday go? I decide to walk up the hill towards Billy's house. It feels like summer again and the swallows dive about me. Billy's vehicle is not there; I think he's away with Nigel, and Bill's kennel is empty too. It's just the peace I want. Then Ben's face shows nervously from his kennel, but when he sees it's me, he smiles.

I smile back, then take a breath and venture, 'Can we go back, back to that terrible day; has anything more come back to you?' Ben turns and starts to walk away, and I'm afraid I've upset him. 'I'm sorry', I say, 'I know it's painful, but I really think you might be able to help solve this mystery.' He stops, turns and faces me.

'When I found my Master, I thought he had tripped, that he would sit up at any moment and speak softly to me, as he always did. I heard someone moving away, beyond the hedge, then he stopped and bent down as if to pick something up. He must have heard me panting, because he moved away quickly, nearly running, stumbling a little.'

'Why didn't you go after him?' I ask.

'Yes, perhaps I should have, but I didn't know what had happened. I still expected my master to get up and for all to be well.'

'So, you have no idea who it was that crept away beyond the hedge?'

'No - except for his cap.'

'What about his cap?'

'It was different.' Ben pauses, trying to find the right words. 'A funny tartan, different to my master's. It was very bright, sort of red.' He stops again, then becomes excited. 'Yes - his cap was full of red!'

15

It's the first day of September and we are holding our first partridge day in the new place. We are excited, but the efforts of the last few days are catching up with us and thoughts of what Ben said fill my mind. Do I know a man with red in his tweed? Is this related to the gun with the dark-coloured patch? Will I see someone walking out today to answer these questions?

We wind our way along country roads for several minutes before we leave the heat of the tarmac and head off and upwards towards the moor. We take a bend to the left and the lunch hut is on the right. It is a stout wooden building with a stone chimney and a strange pot on the top that looks like a duck landing.

I'm soon deep in the valley with Nigel, and Kate is with Billy. The river has bitten a deep gorge through the peat, right down to the rock. Birds come with the breeze, some on their own, and some in coveys. As I wait for the next ones to appear, the wind seems to pick up and blows the beauty of this small valley into focus. A bird comes into view and glides away, but another falls into the burn, and I retrieve it as it floats downstream. As we return to the wooden hut, I cast my eyes around the guests once more. All are in tweed, some mostly blue, some green, but none with red.

The day goes well enough and it's a happy Nigel who leaps from the vehicle as we arrive back at the castle, with the sun shining brightly. Bees are enjoying the blossom in Tim's garden, everything is enjoying the sunshine, sunshine that I hope will still be here next week. Tim is not in his garden, but the house door is ajar, so I push my way in. I start to tell him about the day, but he can sense my mind is elsewhere, and I know this is not what he wants to talk about.

'Which day are you coming over to the lawn?' I ask, as though the day is all that remains to be agreed. Wednesday, Sarah says, if the sun shines, at three. I leave straight away, saying I must help with the guests, but really, I am too excited for that. I must make sure everything is right for Wednesday.

😺

It's a bright and sunny morning as I inspect the grounds - their first thorough inspection for too long. Tim will be here tomorrow, and everything must be perfect. Kate helps me clear my tree camp, which has filled with leaves and dirt. I make sure the jewellery is safely hidden and jog over towards the compound where Nigel is still working. Then a strong scent of rabbit stops me and draws me into the storage shed nearby. It is full of folding tables and stacking chairs, discarded pictures and seldom used cups. In the corner, some old golf clubs are covered by a tattered curtain, but the scent takes me there, and I snatch away the curtain with my teeth. A young rabbit slips past me and out of the door. I should have caught him, but my attention is elsewhere. Something is standing out among the golf clubs, of a different height and colour. It's the shotgun with the dark-coloured patch on the stock! Why is it here and who moved it from the gun room? I think back to my glimpse of Gwen moving something from her car under the chestnut tree. Could it have been this gun? Whose is it? Could it have belonged to my body?

Tim arrives with Sarah just before three the next day, and Kate and I are waiting. I have been hoping for sunshine all week and my wish is granted. Nigel has mown the lawns, and the smell of freshly cut grass fills the air. I lead the way to my tree camp, run in erratic circles and bark with excitement. Even though the sun is warm, Tim is well wrapped up in a woollen jumper and zip-up coat and, despite his efforts to be cheerful, I sense a growing pain. It is slowly gnawing away at him till he ceases to be the same Tim and becomes a mixture of anger and sadness. This is what he tells me as we sit by the scraggy pine that protects my hideaway. He asks me not to tell his mother, though I know she knows. I want to take him with me to my camp. My world below ground where there is no pain, just fun and laughter!

I tell him about the day at partridge and mention all the bits that are exciting but that I could not remember earlier. Kate and I run in the wild area behind the lake and make a rabbit bolt past him. All this happens as he sits silently, and his mother stands with a sorrowful look on her face. I want today to be so good, so happy, so much a sign that tomorrow will be a part of his recovery, yet I know that cannot be. Nigel and Gwen join us for tea and cake as the autumn sun sinks in the west. I see the world sinking too but can do nothing about it.

Tim has gone back home to rest - he tires so quickly - and Kate joins me as I hide in my bed. I come here when nowhere else will do, and she knows it. She wants to talk. I don't want to listen but know I must.

'The wedding is to be in November, I heard Gwen telling Susan a few minutes ago.'

I am shocked. Shocked because this will be in the middle of the pheasant season, and how will Nigel find the time; but also, because it is so soon. It means Gwen is reeling him in. He is a cornered pheasant with a terrier about to grasp his tail!

Tomorrow comes and I have never been so pleased to go on a sporting day with the rain pouring down. Partridge in the rain are hard work, but today it could only improve my mood. Later, I can hardly remember the morning and only recall the afternoon because it included the retrieving of an especially difficult bird, which had become wedged in the burn below a rough, overhanging rock. We are all relieved when our guests leave; yesterday on the lawn, followed by today's sport has exhausted us all.

And so, it is Friday. I leave the cottage with Nigel at eight. Yesterday's rain has gone, but the air is still heavy and water drips freely from the trees. A pair of wood pigeon burst from the big Douglas fir beside the marquee and fly either side of the lime tree that borders it.

I stand here and look across the lawn, my lawn, the lawn I take for granted as being a permanent part of my chaotic life. I find it difficult not to imprint Tim on my picture and, although I know he isn't here today, I am scared to remove him in case he never comes back.

All this time, Ben's comments about the cap with a red tartan have niggled in my mind. It meant little at the time, and still does, but I know it is significant. I mentioned it to Kate, but she just looked away as if I was wasting her time with more irrelevant details. Anyway, I have stored it in my memory. If it matters, I will be ready!

Saturday's sporting party arrives just before dinner and I run to the door, introducing myself to a rather odd dog called Colin. He is similar to the pointers, but with long, unruly hair, a longer nose and the longest eyebrows in the world. He is halfway across the lawn when I see him and, at first, I think he is stalking a rabbit - but there is no rabbit. He looks one way when he is really seeing another and, when he walks, I think he's about to trip over but he never quite does. All in all, he is most unusual. I really look forward to working with him tomorrow!

The moor is bathed in mist, and we are forced to do some of the lower ground where we can see a safe distance. We are five dogs today: Colin, Bill, the fat Labrador called Rory, Kate and me. I look for Ben and had hoped he would be here so we could have continued our talk, but there is no sign.

Colin describes himself as an Irish Setter and is upset when I liken him to a pointer. However, this is the only thing on which we disagree. He comes from what he calls 'the North' and seems to have worked everywhere, and for many years. I believe, being Irish, he is gifted at telling tales but decide that a tall tale well told is better than the truth told badly!

At lunchtime I move outside to enjoy the sun. An Irishman called Patrick comes out too and takes a box of cartridges from Nigel's Land Rover. As he does so he leans his gun against the vehicle door and my mind freezes. I have a blurred memory of a gun against a vehicle in the same yard. Why is it blurred? It's the snow, yes, the memory is of the snow! I ask my eyes to focus on the gun through the swirling blizzard. Can I see the stock, does it have a mahogany-coloured patch? Yes, yes it does, and who is with it, can I see? A man lifts the gun and slides it into its protective sleeve. I strive to see him, his face. My eyes are watering, the snow is swirling and people around me are moving; lunch must be over. I am about to release the dream when the man takes the cap from his head and taps it on the vehicle to shake off the snow. Suddenly the tweed is there as sharp as the sharpest day - Joe's tweed! I feel disappointment. I want it to be a tartan that's full of red, but the image I have just seen was a memory of the victim, the man who became my body. When I see the red tartan, will I see the murderer?

🐾

While I enjoy moorland sport, the heather can literally be a pain. My legs are not long enough, and when I'm constantly springing forward to see what's happening in the long heather, it rubs them badly. In cool weather I can ease them in a burn, but when it's warm, they become sore and attract the flies like a dead rabbit.

'Do you think Gwen and Ian are still lovers?' Kate says, looking directly at me, wanting to see the answer in my eyes. I look up from my sore legs.

'I'm sure they are. I believe Gwen only wants Nigel for what he has, for all this', I reply, with a nod towards the castle.

'And when she has it?' Kate asks.

'Then she'll find some reason to dump him and enjoy her share with Ian.'

Kate takes a deep breath and looks across the valley.

'Am I not right?' I demand.

Her eyes move to some distant point across the valley, then back to me and say that I'm right. 'We must think of a way to spoil things.'

'And before November', I add chirpily.

'Yes, before November.'

I want to talk about the gun, and now seems the perfect time.

'You know I saw Gwen take a gun from her car some weeks ago', I say in a matter-of-fact way. 'And later I saw a strange gun amongst Nigel's collection.'

She doesn't answer but gives me that 'it's news to me' look. I continue.

'Well, that gun is now sitting amongst the old golf clubs in the storage shed, and I'm sure it's the one that my man - the man who became a body - used.'

Kate still doesn't speak, but I know I have hit home. I look across the valley. After a pause, she says,

'I'm not sure about this walked up grouse shooting, what do you think?'

So, Gwen, Ian and the gun have been filed for now.

'It's certainly harder work', I reply, 'and I'm annoyed when guests think they are so much fitter than they really are, and the return is few birds for all the effort. But it gives me a great chance to work the moor, to hunt where I wouldn't usually go - to escape the castle and truly be myself. I can see for miles from the hill, and I can certainly think better up there!'

Kate seems unimpressed and moves away towards the castle, and I wonder what she really means. I'm sure it has little to do with grouse shooting and more to do with not having an answer about the gun.

So, Gwen is to marry Nigel, when she really wants Ian. We have a gun hidden in the storage shed, a cartridge bag in the wrong place, a whistle where it shouldn't be and a cap that belongs to two men and no one. And the red tartan, we mustn't forget that! I roll over in my bed and close my eyes Time for sleep!

16

We have all - and I'm speaking as a member of the wedding team here - really got the hang of weddings. Tim has never been to one of ours, though he has seen and heard many from his garden. I see him there now, resting in his chair, as I lead a group of children on a tour and then organise a game for them. Today's wedding has filled my day, and its guests will soon be eating in the marquee.

It's a big wedding, bigger than normal, with nearly two hundred guests and twenty children. I can hear them now, as they grow bored at the table and start to run around noisily on the marquee's wooden floor.

I enjoy a quiet spot under the reception desk, till the sounds of washing pans and running water drive me into the small office. I must have fallen sleep, because I am started by the sound of Ian's voice. He's been away and wants an update.

'The twentieth of November', says Gwen. 'Small and in the chapel.'

'So, he's accepted you're pregnant. Can you feign some morning sickness or something? It won't take much to convince him, and the baby wouldn't be showing by then.' Gwen agrees and makes off for the marquee, where the band is warming up.

Oliver is still away, so Nigel is doing his work, and I know he is finding it tiring. I am not surprised! He has hosted all the extra guest days and tried to help with weddings too! Gwen has been no help. She has been using her 'pregnancy' to hide away and, I'm sure, to meet up with Ian.

In the morning, Nigel drives up the valley to see some cows and calves that are grazing around the loch, and I have come to help. It's weeks since I've been here and, although I have little interest in cows, and even less when they have calves and are likely to chase me with their heads down and horns waving, I'm glad to be here. We are at the top of the loch, my view is interrupted by the many thorn bushes that grow there, and Nigel is resting on a fallen hazel bough. He is looking for a cow and its calf but doesn't want to climb up the shale covered ground, so, I offer to go.

Something hovers over me; it's the peregrine. Its family has nested here for years, and I am so distracted that I almost bump into the calf that's rubbing against a bush whilst its mother stands and swishes her tail. I quickly turn back; I've done my job.

Nigel's rest has done him some good, but he still has rings around his eyes. He looks better when he smiles, and for that I know he needs Sarah.

It's another day, and every new day seems to bump into the last. We have another party of guests and are travelling to the new ground. A haze follows us down the road. Why do I keep mentioning the heat? Because it eats into everything I do, sucking my energy and dulling my mind! I look forward to lying in the burn there. Will the breeze be blowing up the valley, as I know it can? I doze, till the bumpy road to the meeting hut wakes me.

I recognise some of the guests as soon as I hop down, as well as Meg, a Springer Spaniel, who comes with her very tall owner. This is the party that come several times a year; the ones who moan when they miss their target as if it's our fault!

I am suddenly thinking of the cartridge bag, the one Kate found down the valley from my body and which I recognised as belonging to Hamish, today's team captain. Perhaps he's not coming today, I haven't seen him. Then suddenly a car arrives at speed, throwing dust over everything. Without looking I know it's him. Everyone is shouting, telling him he's late again. He steps slowly out of his car - he likes to be important and is revelling in everyone's attention.

He strides into the wooden building, wearing his awful tartan, and claims a coffee, which I know will irritate Nigel as he is keen to move off.

Hamish's car door has not closed properly, and the breeze pushes it open. A sheet of paper blows out and across the road. I leap up, grab it and carry it to the shelter of the log store at the back. Nigel is calling me, so I push it behind a log for now, but not before I glimpse a colourful crest at the top of the paper. It is the same crest I saw on the paper in Jane's dead hand!

My brain starts to whirl, but I must put this new development out of my head for now – there are partridge to be retrieved.

The party will be shooting at partridge for the first time. I remember how difficult they found the pheasants - how they moaned – and fear the worst for today. Partridge are smaller than pheasant and can turn quickly in the air. Will the challenge be too much?

But, for now, the team are in the hut, drinking coffee and drawing lots, while I'm enjoying the shade of the veranda and the company of Kate and Meg. The moor stretches out to the distance and the horizon is a haze of purples and greens. I know the scent won't be good today - the heat will have killed it!

The men take their time, and when they do emerge, I'm ready for the short walk to where we normally start. I can already taste the cool burn water in my mouth, but see we are heading along the road and into a cloud of dust. We are clearly starting up on the moor and I follow, trying to look keen.

We leave the road and take a winding path through the heather till we come to a line of hollows in the ground, each with a low stone wall. These, I know, are called butts and they hide the men from the oncoming birds. Kate suddenly comes to life, following keenly as Nigel and I lead a guest to the third butt, where I lie, with the butt giving me shade and the heather a pillow. Kate finds herself the only bush to hide behind and Meg is in the butt below us; I can see her mainly white body as she shades behind a large rock.

The heather is tall and restricts my view, but I can see the beaters in the distance and hear the crack of their flags. I hear shots from the butt above me and then a flash of something flying low and very fast across my front. Soon, birds are coming from every side. Guns fire till the whistle blows and peace returns, then Kate leaps into life as I have seldom seen her.

'This is just how I remember it!' is the only explanation she gives as she crosses our path and disappears into the heather.

Ben is helping today. He's been with Billy, and I've only just seen him. He is shaking, but why? I lead him behind a now deserted butt.

'Look', he stammers, pointing towards Hamish, who is walking towards us with a ruddy glow on his face and a brace of birds in his hand.

'That's the cap I saw through the hedge when my master died! As he bent down, I saw it!'

Ben retreats into the heather and away from the man he sees as the murderer. Hamish walks past me, leans on the wall of the butt and removes the cap from his sweaty brow. It matches the rest of his outfit, awful and garish! Throughout it is a broad orange stripe.

'Well, Ben, if you want to call it red that's fine by me', I think. I am just a metre from him; am I really this close to a killer?

Later, back at the castle, Kate tosses and turns all night, frequently reliving what has clearly been a very exciting day for her. Meanwhile, I lie still, thinking on the letter and what it means. Who had Hamish written to, and why was the note bearing his crest in Jane's hand? Were Gwen and Ian involved, or is Hamish alone the villain? Or was Jane's death simply a coincidence and the note unimportant? No, the note matters, I'm sure! The police think Jane's husband killed her so did he know Hamish? No answers come, but as sleep sweeps over me my thoughts have settled on one thing, Hamish has questions to answer!

Hot day rolls into hot day, and the next morning Kate and I lie stretched out in the shade of the cedar tree. I finally tell her about the letter blowing from Hamish's car and she sits up sharply.

'There was something about Hamish that was important, but I couldn't place it', she says, then looks at me, wanting me to guess what it is.

'And now you can?', I prompt.

'Do you remember when Joe and I came to help you with a day before Christmas last year? It was one of Hamish's days.'

I admit that I don't.

'I remember him clearly; he was speaking with Gwen. And it must have been at the lunch hut because they don't come to the castle, do they?'

'Not usually', I agree. 'But why was Gwen at the lunch hut?' We look at each other.

'Perhaps she was helping Sarah transport the lunch?', suggests Kate.

'Or maybe Nigel had forgotten something, and she went to get it for him?', I add. Neither of us are convinced and I see Kate adding Hamish to her list of suspects.

A young girl, called Linda, is looking for me. She came to a wedding last year, when it was cool, and I was full of energy, and she wants to know why I don't want to play now. Eventually, my pride wins over my exhaustion, and I take Linda to my camp. Even here the flies buzz and the leaves droop, but every now and then a wisp of breeze from the lake reaches me and I feel alive again. We play, with Linda throwing a stone as far under the trees as she can, and me retrieving it to howls of laughter. When she goes, I return to the castle and look for Nigel.

I find him in the gun room, where he has been pretending to count cartridges, but I know he has really been hiding. I sense a change in him. Has it to do with the farm or the castle; his pending wedding with Gwen or Jane's sudden death? Is it concerning the sport up the valley, something that directly concerns me? I am close to Nigel. He tells me things he tells no one else, and I see things others don't, yet I still don't know! I look into his eyes, as I do with a fellow dog, and today Nigel's are troubled.

The new ground has gone well enough, as have the grouse on the old one, but a new month is here. All is different; this is the pheasant season. The days of relaxed walking across the moor, when exercise and scenery are important, will soon be behind us and guests will come for high birds and formality. I want to believe it is this that troubles him, but he carries a weight I haven't seen before, and it scares me!

🐾

'They've done it; they brought it forward. They're married!'

'They've done what?' I stand, shocked and speechless. Kate takes a breath and continues.

'Gwen told Nigel they had a cancellation at the Registry Office and that it would fit his diary better to wed sooner rather than later.'

'So, they just went off and did it?' I whisper. 'Now she's got everything she wanted.' I look at Kate, feeling hopeless.

'They've gone away for the night. Nigel will meet us at the lunch hut in the morning.'

We walk back to the castle together. We will have to host the guests as they arrive, and they will be excited by the news. Everyone will be excited, except us!

Our first day at pheasant is only a small day, with few guests and few men with dogs to run it. It is the ultimate in relaxed, down to earth sport. There is no formality, no need for me to be on duty; just four men with three of us dogs, and a whole day for us to enjoy. Kate is with us in body, though I know this is not her type of day. She will take part and do her bit, but her dreams are already with the first of the big days that start next week.

Nick and Arthur, our guests, arrived smartly. Sarah has brought Kate and I down and she will do the lunch, but she is unusually quiet, and I know her thoughts are on the wedding. Nigel rushes in and accepts everyone's congratulations, but he looks more like a lost sheep than a top dog to me.

The sun is shining as we leave the neat fields and head towards the moorland. I think we will start next to a wood and walk away uphill, but we start so far out that I sense there will be very few pheasant and just the odd elusive rabbit. I am right; we walk for ages, only find three rabbits and shoot none.

It's well past lunch time when we return to our vehicles, very hot and with a miserable two rabbits to show for all our efforts. We lunch in the old barn, where Billy has lit a fire for us and, although it's hot, we're pleased as Nick can dry his shirt, which is soaked with sweat.

In the afternoon, we head up a small side valley with steep, bracken-covered banks and rushes in the bottom. The men find the walking hard, till Nigel shows them an old sheep path that winds its way around the trees. It should make their shooting easier, though by the way they have missed the rabbits before lunch, I'm not too sure.

A pheasant flies forwards, and then more follow. Soon they will want to fly home to the wood behind us and I picture them taking off high in front of me and curling round over Nick and Arthur in the valley below. Suddenly, one does exactly that, two more follow, and Nigel sends me down to help find the birds. I have mine and can see Belle with hers, then Kate appears with another - what a team we are! Nigel takes the bird from me, and I lie in the burn, letting the cool water flow over me. I wonder if there can be anywhere in the world better than this, with the sun shining, the birds flying and the cool water flowing.

When we reach the top of the valley, we turn and head back towards the wood. Arthur makes a good shot, and a pheasant falls into the bracken well up the hill. I am pleased for Arthur, but not for me, as I will have to fetch it. I fall as much as walk down that wretched slope and then lie in the burn again, panting. Nigel is amused and laughs. You wouldn't be laughing if you had just fetched it, I think!

We are back at the lunch barn, and everyone is happy now - far happier than this morning. But my attention is drawn to a car parked just down the road, between us and Billy's cottage. I remember it arriving at the new ground, late and surrounded by a cloud of dust and I wasn't expecting to see it today. I hear the voices of Billy and Hamish coming from Billy's garden, and creep nearer. I can't pick out their words, but their talk is not the relaxed talk of sportsmen. As I move closer, Nigel's voice echoes down the road. He is calling me, and the sound brings silence from Billy and Hamish. I walk back towards the lunch hut and hear Billy close his gate and follow me. Hamish drives away.

'How did it go? I heard plenty of shooting from up the valley', calls Billy as he approaches us. He is trying to be humorous, but humour and Billy do not go together. The party laugh, yet I know Billy is uncomfortable. Is that because he fears we have disturbed too many of his birds, or because we returned before Hamish left? Is he worried we might have heard what they were saying?

As I lie on my sofa that evening, I dream of many things; a mixture of Kate and Meg and the big day to come; of dear Tim, who will never feel the joy of days like these. And, interrupting them all, is that awful orange stripe and a persisting image of Hamish.

In the morning, I walk over to Tim and tell him of the first small day at pheasant. I feel pathetic! How can I keep telling him the same things, things he has never done and can barely understand? If I were him, would I want to hear about them? I want to tell him something exciting that will bring us together in every way but, sadly, I know there is no such thing. I look up and his eyes are laughing. How can he laugh when he has nothing but my love and second-hand stories?

17

I sleep a broken sleep, and I can't blame it on the heat. Sometimes the valley shouts to me, even from the high hill when my mind is fixed on the grouse or pheasant. I know I've been excited by the start of the season - you can probably tell! - and that soon I will be even busier. Thoughts of it make me smile, but I mustn't be distracted. Inside, I know that if I don't solve the mystery, it may destroy my sport and what it means to me.

Today I get my chance. Nigel and Billy are discussing the sporting days for next week and before I know it, the rushes are brushing my nose and my feet are cooling in the marsh water. Perhaps Hamish has brought everything to a head! Everything in the valley is very green, but my mind becomes full of white; whiteness seems to shout, but what is it saying? I look at the spot where I found the body. It is etched on my mind, as are the tracks on the grass field that have now disappeared behind the summer grass. It is these tracks that I find most unsettling. Why, what is so wrong?

When we arrive back at the castle, I lie down, tired, and close my eyes. Again, the day of the murder comes as a dream, but not as before. I see faces laughing and joking and I try to focus on them. I want to look into their eyes. Perhaps the face of the victim will come back to me, and maybe even that of the murderer! Yet, however hard I look, their faces are still hidden.

They are loading up now, saying their farewells, and everything grows darker and even less clear, and I fear it's the 'cloud'. I shake my head. Something is weighing on it and I know it's the snow, mountains of it. They are all leaving quickly, leaping into their cars and making off. Only the snow remains - and suddenly I know what is wrong! Nobody could have driven down to the murder spot now, even if they knew the way. Whatever those tracks were, they were not made around the time of the murder.

I know I must think again.

🐾

The first full day at pheasant is tomorrow, and the guests are arriving. Nigel takes them to the gun room, to store their weapons, and I lie in the bar where the early arrivals are enjoying a drink. I sense a difference to the days that have gone before, and Nigel settles into his pre-big day ritual. He walks with a confidence I rarely see, and I know it's not real. He looks and smiles at the guests, but not at me. He knows he can't fool me! On the surface, all is relaxed banter and jokes, yet we all know that tomorrow we will have to perform better than we have all season.

Everyone is talking about Jane and her vicious murder. It sends a clear chill through the conversation. Nigel has said they think it was her husband, and they shake their heads, but they still have thoughts of a wicked killer hovering behind every tree. My body is not mentioned and I'm sure everyone has accepted it was an accident. This is good! Perhaps the murderer will relax and give away their identity.

There are three dogs staying: two Cocker Spaniels, who I meet briefly, and a big Labrador, who seems so old I don't think he sees me as he waddles up to his master's room.

As you know, I am not really a 'big day' dog. Fortunately, Nigel will be working with me, and having placed the guests, he will take me to the end of the line - or behind it, where there are no other dogs - and give me a free rein to find the birds. Often, we will return with more in our bag than some in the middle of the line, but, being a modest dog, I seldom mention it. Kate is happy too. A friend of Joe's is shooting and has asked if she can work for him. She loves sitting in the line, but I know she's worried.

'Do you know, this will be my first real day in the line since Joe died?'

I try to imagine losing Nigel and how my next day would feel!

'You'll be fine', I say, and know she will be.

My mind is racing now; the day will be awesome. Billy has worked, as I have told you, from back in the spring, to grow the birds to be strong and wild, to make their home in the highest woods and to place the guests where the challenge will be as difficult as possible. That has been his job; mine will be to flush them and retrieve them, as the guests bag as many as they can from the birds that streak high and fast over their heads. I shake my head, stretch as much as my basket will allow and then curl up to get some much-needed rest.

I wake before dawn and hear Nigel moving upstairs. Our busy day is beginning! After an early breakfast, everyone assembles in the yard. Some of the picking up dogs have come for the first time this season and they are sniffing about, trying to look important and raring to go.

At lunch, we catch up on all the news and Kate is full of how well her man is doing. Most of the other dogs seem to have heard of my adventure with the car, and know about Joe's death, and the body. Like everyone, they have accepted that they were accidents. How will they react when we show they were not? I glance across at Kate, feeling like a conspirator who needs reassurance, but she is still talking about the morning.

We all like to think we haven't changed since last year, though some of the Labradors have certainly aged. One guest has a new, young dog that is very overconfident and rushes into the cattle barn, barking. I retrieve him and try to calm him down by explaining my role at the castle - the guests, the weddings, the duties on the lawn and the children - but he doesn't seem to pay much attention or understand what I am saying. Only Jack, an old golden Labrador, shows any interest.

I first met Jack when I was a very young dog in my first season. I watched him as a pheasant fell into the end of a wood but, instead of going in after it, he gently trotted across, entered the wood halfway down and very soon came out with the bird. Very impressed, as a keen young dog can be, I asked him how he knew? He just smiled.

'Watch, think and remember and you will know.' And he was right.

We are coming to the end of this, our first full day at pheasant. I am lying under a tree with a wood behind me, the valley in front, and Nigel by my side. I am glad for the rest. The day has given me more retrieves than all the season so far and I am exhausted. I hear Billy and his team in the distance; they will be a few minutes yet.

Everything suddenly looks very beautiful, as if I have just released myself from total concentration and can now see the wood for the trees. The leaves on the beech trees vary from yellow, through gold to red, whilst the spruce retain their dark, healthy, spiky, green. The hills, where we walked for grouse just days ago, are topped with snow and the grass still shines with frost where the sun hasn't reached. I picture the evening when men will tease men about birds that got away, or recount heroic shots that should have been impossible - and I will know that most of them were!

Then I see the body and the tracks running down to it. They are there and go to just above where I found the body. But not then, not when the man died in the middle of a blizzard. So, how did the man get there, how did the murderer get there, and how did he escape?

Although there have been frosts out on the moor, I wake to our first real frost down at the castle. Everything glistens in the sun and the lake has a thin cobweb of ice on it. The oldest Labrador, whose name is Jumbo, is on the lawn and seriously suffering from yesterday, though I can't remember him doing very much. I walk up to him and make sure he knows about the frozen lake. I doubt he would have the energy to get in, let alone out, but feel responsible.

The guests all gather on my lawn, and the two Cocker Spaniels, Jim and Fred, run around as only Cockers can. The ache in my leg has returned. My mind seems full of dogs, and this makes me smile, but the ache remains - and more so after real exercise. I suddenly feel older. I know there is only one way to cheer myself, and crawl under the fence.

Tim is looking out of his big sliding windows and enjoying the sun without the cold. For a while, we both just sit and look out at the brilliance of the sun on the frosted ground. Sometimes silence is the best way, even for Tim and me. I can sense a flow of satisfaction that has come with this morning and its natural beauty, and don't want to disturb it. After a time, I move and lie right next to Tim. I feel his hand touching my back. My leg continues to ache, but I know I can't possibly be in as much pain as him, and I try to ignore it. His mother comes in and our silent spell is broken. They are going out, another trip to the hospital, and I wish him well.

I take myself and my thoughts to the castle sitting room. The flames jump and bounce their glow off the copper-topped table, and I test the carpet beside it. It's as soft as I remember, and the warmth feels good.

The next party isn't due for a few days, and my mind can't escape Tim. He has been spending a lot of time at the hospital and I am very aware that's not a good sign. I find it difficult to relax, even on my sofa, and take to wandering the castle.

I stand on the first-floor landing, where I wait during a very foody dinner, and look about. I'm the only one here and wander into the dining room. The table is laid, the carpet cleaned, and the sun is leaving a mist of floating dust as it bursts through the large windows. I have never thought anything could dent my enthusiasm for a day out in the woods, or up the river, but today I'm pleased to be here, inside. I wonder if this is the first sign of growing old, or the effect of a sore leg when I have, until now, known so little pain. Or perhaps it is simply that I am thinking of Tim and have realised that little of what I do really matters.

I settle on my sofa and as the sun moves in the sky, its rays land on me. I want the warmth to relax me, but there's a tension that persists. I know that, even when everything else settles, the cunning of Gwen and Ian is ever-present. Nigel still hasn't spoken of his wedding. Gwen has been away, or has been hiding herself well, and Ian has disappeared into the background. He's good at that! I can't help but wonder what they will do now.

Kate has gone with Nigel and Gwen in the Land Rover. I don't know where! Normally it wouldn't matter, but Gwen is increasingly annoying, and Kate is especially full of herself at the moment. Kate seems to see Tim's death as a certainty and cannot understand my refusal to accept that his end is near.

'So, what is Gwen up to?', I ask Kate when she returns. I hope she has used her trip to test the water, to find answers.

'She is still after her new house. She talks about it as if it's hers now, and I think she'll get it.'

I think of the lovely spot. The trees, the valley, the glorious birds that fly from one side to the other, and how a new house would spoil it all!

'And Ian, what of him?', I ask.

'Ah, yes, I overheard him speaking with Gwen this morning', Kate replies, chirpily. 'They are still together and are more relaxed now. They plan to meet whilst Nigel is away with guests next week.'

'Do they?' I whisper to myself!

An ambulance comes along the road, still hidden behind the tall hedge, which is only now beginning to shed its summer leaves and turns down Tim's driveway. When Tim emerges, I see he is wrapped in more clothes than I have ever seen on a man, but his face is partially visible, and his eyes are looking for me. He disappears indoors and I follow. Sarah has a tired look on her face, and I know to lie quietly by Tim's feet. No one has the energy for excitement.

🐾

After too many quiet days, I am ready for action! I am on the old sack in Nigel's Land Rover and the freedom feels good. We are leading the way along the farm track on our way to the next drive. The same party were here yesterday and, by the noise, were still enjoying themselves well into the night. Nigel was quiet this morning and I think he has a headache, but he was up early to see the cattle. I walked out with him and the sky was as dark as it could be, with no stars or moon to light it. He let me run around the hen field as the sun burst above the horizon, then wait by the gate as the cows walked up for their feed. I know he enjoyed me being there, though there was little I could do to help. What you need, I thought, as we returned to ready ourselves for the sporting day ahead, is a young Gunner. Someone who is bred to look after cattle and sheep, and someone for me to talk to when Kate is annoying!

My leg is aching, and we are only half-way to lunchtime. The guests are happily drinking soup from small beakers and laughing. I am lying on the track and lapping water from a muddy puddle, thinking how good it tastes. Do I have the energy to get back in the Land Rover, I wonder?

The day drifts on, but before the sun sets, it is over, and the guests have gone. I think they enjoyed their day, but I can't remember how it finished. Why am I so tired? Come on Mutley, it's time to wake up!

In the morning, Billy drives off with Kate sitting nervously in the back of his vehicle. I am resting. They are hosting a small day - the kind Billy hates - and my leg is playing up. Kate thinks I'm faking, making a fuss, so she will have to suffer Billy alone. I'm not saying I couldn't have gone if it had been essential, but it will do Kate good to be on her own and I have other plans! Nigel still has Oliver's work to do, and I am helping.

I saw Ian looking at the diary yesterday and as soon as I saw the look on his face, I knew he was checking Nigel's movements. This is my chance - perhaps my only chance - to show Nigel the truth.

We have checked two lots of sheep, the cattle by the loch, and are now with more sheep by the top road. Nigel is in the field. The sheep are to our right, sheltering under the tall conifer wood that grows there and I have run ahead and am waiting by the gate. Nigel has stopped and is breathing hard, looking across the valley. What is he thinking? Does he see the same threat to all this that Kate and I see? I know he is worried. If only he would hurry, I will show him there is hope, that all this will be safe.

Eventually he reaches me, and we drive towards the castle. He hasn't spoken, and I haven't encouraged him; I want us to get back. When we arrive, I run around playfully, making Nigel laugh, and then grab one of his favourite gloves and run off with it towards the cottage. He follows. I bound up the stairs and into his bedroom, sure of what I will find – and there they are! Nigel has followed me, too out of breath to shout, and is now standing, speechless, staring at Gwen and Ian together. I sneak away, expecting loud and angry words to follow, but Nigel dashes after me down the stairs, and we head back to the castle in silence.

I wait by the door, trying to understand what might be in Nigel's head. I knew what I had to do but can hardly believe that I've done it. Could it be so simple? Has Nigel seen the truth? Have I saved the day? I hear noises from upstairs, it must be Gwen. I leave the castle without looking back and make for my retreat under the cedar tree; for once I am a coward.

Yes, Gwen has gone. They - that is, Nigel and Gwen - had several long talks in the cottage that could be heard from my camp by the scraggy pine tree, separated by long gaps that were quieter than waiting for Billy on a bad day. Many people are shocked. They want to know why they have split, and so soon. Nigel has remained silent. Some are saying it was the new house, or the lack of it, and others that Oliver's illness was really the cause – that Gwen could not understand Nigel's commitment to covering for his brother and the fact that someone needed to take on Oliver's work.

Anyway, the important thing is, Gwen has gone and, I believe, so has Ian, so that is that! What did they have to do with my body, or Joe or Jane? Will I ever know? Kate didn't foresee their going in a 'cloud', so perhaps she thinks they weren't that important after all.

Nigel is either burying himself in Oliver's work, which may or may not be necessary, or hiding in the office. Kate is annoyed to have missed it all, and more annoyed that I won't tell her every detail. But my first loyalty is to Nigel, and I owe him my discretion. Kate will just have to lump it.

Today we have another sporting party, and I am overjoyed. It's not that the party is likely to be memorable or the day especially good, but we are away from the castle and Nigel is doing what he likes best. He can control the day, charm the guests, disagree with Billy and suddenly be the Nigel I know and love. The moment we cross the bridge from the castle gardens to the meadows, the chicken field and the woods beyond, he becomes his old self. We are a team again! Should I tell him how much pain I feel in my leg and how much have worried about him? No, this is not the time! The mist clears as he speaks, excuses become unnecessary, and any pain goes.

🐾

'Well, are you coming, we're at Fender tomorrow, if you're up to it?'

It's a small day, just a few miles away, with some of Nigel's friends. There are no Pointers today, nor any other dogs to replace them, so everyone looks to me to find their birds. Nigel doesn't mention that I have been down, or even that I have had an accident; he just assumes I will do what is needed - and I do. The low points of the past few days are gone, and I feel strong again.

I ask my leg how it feels. There is still an ache, but I can handle it. A rabbit springs from a bush nearby and suddenly I have him in my mouth. It is the first rabbit I've caught for a very long time, I'm on the top of the world and can't wait for our next day up the valley tomorrow.

That evening, a large coach draws into the drive loaded with guests. They are all young, both men and women, and I run about them as they walk in the grounds, trying to make them notice me. A girl, with shining eyes and black hair, throws a ball for me and I run after it. I scoop it up in my mouth at speed — what a retrieve! — but as I turn, I feel a terrible pain in my leg, and everything goes dark.

18

I can see myself, very clearly, but in the dark! Where am I? Am I dead; is this how it feels? I'm floating and am afraid I'll be blown away by the breeze. Has anyone noticed? Now I know my body is on the ground. Will someone come and load me up, count me among the bag as just another to be added to the total!

Slowly I regain my senses. I am on the ground where I fell. Sarah is over me and a sea of faces are behind her. I want to get up, but my body won't respond and I'm panicking inside. I hear Sarah raising her voice. Kate is looking down and the faces are being sent away, but I just lie there. Someone wants to lift me, but they stop and put a blanket on me instead.

I want it to be the blanket from my cage, or the old sack. I want to be in my cage, with a full working day in front of me, but I'm not. Again, I ask myself if I am dying. Will I ever run again, pick up a pheasant or fetch a stick?

I sense someone near - so I'm not dead! I recognise a man's voice, which makes me feel better, even though I know it's the vet that usually hurts me. He is touching my leg and although I expect it to hurt, it doesn't. I try to make out what's being said, but all I sense is Kate licking me. The blackness returns.

When I come to, I'm in a big cage. I don't know where, but it's not the castle. I'm still dreaming, drifting, and below me are pictures that are parts of my memory but mixed up. I want to stand up but know I can't. I find my mind analysing my body and asking what I can or can't feel or do. I pluck up the courage to ask my leg to move - and it does! I move it again to make sure, and then again. I must have made a noise because a nurse comes and then the vet. They open my door and tell me to stay still. I drift away once more.

The month comes to an end without me noticing or caring. I continue in a dream, with only brief moments when I know where I am. The leg that has caused me such agony and interrupted my life this time, is the same leg that had been giving me trouble since the accident. I wish I had told Nigel, Sarah or Kate about it sooner, and then perhaps I would be better now. Anyway, I stay with the vet for several days and he carries out more tests, and, no doubt, compares them with the tests he did in the summer.

I come home in the middle of the day and, when I walk, feel no pain, just numbness. I'm dizzy and hope it's still the drugs and not me. Nigel thinks he is being clever by hiding my tablets in rolls of ham, but I don't care. I want to see Tim, but not like this, so I walk slowly out onto my lawn. There is always someone watching me, as if I may fall again, and I wish they would give me time to myself. I need to know what I will be able to do and when but am too scared to ask.

I walk further each day and can sense everyone relaxing more when I'm near, but I'm not the dog I was. And it's not just to do with my leg and the fact that I can't feel it. Do I believe I can still work as I did, or play with children without falling and scaring them? I have taken my whole life for granted, have always assumed that I would work till I dropped in pursuit of a rabbit, or went in my sleep after a very busy day.

When will Nigel take me to the woods? When will he lose that annoying smile that I hadn't noticed before. His talks of rest and 'we will see'. I am becoming more and more frustrated.

Sarah suggests I go to see Tim. I don't wait to be lifted over the fence, as Nigel wants; I force myself under it and go to Tim. He is facing the window, looking out over the autumn garden. The large apple tree is loaded with fruit, and around its base blackbirds and thrushes peck at the many fallen ones. I find it sad that no one has had time to pick the fruit.

I look at Tim, and he is as I had feared. The eyes that so recently shone when they spoke now seem cloudy and reading them is like looking for a rabbit on a misty morning. He is pleased to see me, of course, and Sarah rushes in when she knows I'm there. They all avoid talking about my fall and we just sit, as we have so often before. Tim is watching me, and

I feel that he can identify my pain with his. He knows more pain than I can imagine, yet he still looks at me with compassion and reassurance.

A glow shines through the garden hedge. It has grown almost unnoticed, but now it demands my attention and, as it does, is joined by a shooting flash that bursts into cascades of sparks high above my head. I look towards the fire that is burning by the big beech tree and can pick out the silhouettes of people. I hear voices between the bangs, the whooshes of the fireworks, and the laughter. I wish I could walk over to the fire with Tim and join in the fun, but then a rocket bursts overhead, I see Tim's eyes sparkle in its light, and I know we are fine where we are.

Later, I leave Tim to sleep and return to the castle. The fire is roaring in the sitting room, and I lie beside it. I have found the perfect spot with the flames throwing just the right amount of heat onto my leg.

The panic, anger and surprise I felt after my fall are so different to my thoughts after the accident with the car. Then, it was as though I could pass the blame onto the driver. I could almost pretend no injury had occurred and my rapid return to work had told me this was true. Now, I'm increasingly sure my injured leg is from then. I'm having to accept that I am no longer in control and, for the first time in my life, my body is not doing as I tell it. Well, my body may be misbehaving, but my mind wants action, so I settle down and give it the mystery.

I imagine the rug between me and the fire as a holding area, somewhere to line up all the clues and make them fit. I have the body and the dead pheasant; Joe's death; Hamish's cartridge bag and cap and Nigel's whistle. Then there are the tracks that run down to the murder scene; the gun that has been hidden with the old golf clubs; Jane's murder and Hamish's letter. Yes, what about dear Hamish? Does the order matter? I decide it must, and work from there.

I sigh; this is difficult. I know when we found things, but not necessarily when they were put or lost there! I think of the whistle that was Nigel's spare, the one that hung in the lunch hut. I think of cartridge bags and caps, guns, Hamish and the snow! The snow holds the answer, I am sure!

An elderly couple have joined me by the fire, and I pretend to be asleep. Sarah has shown them in and is talking, both about me and to me, and eventually I cannot help wagging my tail. I get up and accept their attention. Sarah has told them about my injury, so they give me extra sympathy, which I pretend to enjoy.

I find it easy to dream about days gone by but try to stop myself. Such dreams are for old dogs that have nothing positive to plan for today or tomorrow and only memories and imaginings to keep them going. I will not accept this! I must believe that each day my leg will improve, and that once again I will sprint across the lawn and work the woods.

The guests have moved to the dining room for their lunch and the fire has died down, so I get up and move to the reception. I have been denied the sofa since my fall and see my return to it as one of the next markers on my road to recovery.

We have a little snow today, which I would love to run in, but Nigel is being silly again and says I might slip. I am tired of sitting by the fire, listening to visiting dogs tell me of their day as if I have never been on one, and never will. The numbness in my leg has been replaced by a dull ache and, if I try hard enough, some real pain. You may think it strange that I want to feel pain but, I can assure you, it's preferable to feeling nothing. Numbness is nothing which is very close to death, or so I have told myself. But to feel pain is a sign of life and is the first step to feeling no pain, and then to recovery.

When everyone is busy, I walk across the lawn and into the rough ground behind. A rabbit tries to tempt me into running, but I resist and stop for a drink from the lake. It looks very inviting and suddenly I'm in the water. It's high, the rushes have died back for the winter, and it feels wonderful. It has started snowing again, and I can feel the soft touch of flakes landing on me as I swim. I am elated, the ache is dulled by the cool water and only when I ask my long-neglected legs to lift me clear of it do I feel a flinch of pain. I stand panting on the lawn and wonder how I am going to explain my wetness! Soon I am by the fire and steaming, a towel is round me, and Sarah is pretending to tell me off.

I fall into a deep sleep that lasts right through the night and into the morning. My exhilarating swim in the lake exhausted me and I realise I still have some recuperating to do. When I wake, Kate is still in her bed. There can be no party out today, or Kate would have left with Nigel long ago. She has been filling in for me and I am pleased that neither she nor Nigel have told me how things have gone. Of course, part of me wants to know which woods are producing the birds, and which new dogs are pulling their weight; but the biggest part knows I will miss it more if I am constantly reminded of it. I hear bits of news from visiting guests, and their dogs cannot resist telling me what I'm missing, but I simply ignore them and concentrate on my recovery. For now, having seen that Kate is sleeping, and snoring comfortably, I roll over.

A new morning and Nigel is away with Kate. They will have a difficult day with snow everywhere and a party that struggles even in good weather, so will be full of excuses. I am on my sofa - yes, I am allowed now. I am enjoying the silence and, for once, grateful to be where I am.

Again, my mind is pulled to the valley, to the memory of the body and all that I have discovered about it. Some makes sense and has come together. The man was certainly mistaken for Joe and killed as such. The killer went down the field to where he knew the man and his dog, Ben, were looking for a wounded bird and once the murder had been committed, he crept away, back up the field to the road. This all fits well, but what about the loose ends? I put all these other facts together, lay them out in my mind, as on a table, and look for another answer.

The killer walked down, and the killer walked back; the snow made anything else impossible. But how did the man who became the body get there? I try to remember what Ben said. Did they walk into the valley or drive some of the way? They came alone, I am sure of that and, as they were guests, it is likely they drove as far as they could. I think of the blizzard and the weather that had gone before. Was the killer someone who knew the valley, or a stranger? A stranger might have driven right down if he was desperate enough and retrieved the vehicle later. But is this likely, or could someone we haven't thought of, a fellow guest on that day perhaps, be the killer?

My mind drifts and settles on Hamish. I like the idea of the killer being a stranger, and I include Hamish here because it excuses the home team - the people I have grown to know and love.

A conference party arrives, led by a jovial man called David. I remember him because he introduces me to his team as if I were a man, before he introduces them to Nigel. I am described as, 'a working dog with a temporary injury', and I love the words.

In the morning, David and his team are on the lawns and a man with various hawks and falcons is displaying them. I follow them out and Nigel lets me go. I feel stiff, a legacy of my recent swim, but am determined not to show it. A very large bird sits on a low perch and wherever I go he looks at me. He has a large, round face with small, sharp ears and feathers sticking out. A smaller version sometimes flies from the top wood; I have seen it often, but I am uncomfortable with this bird and retreat to the bar.

My fitness will only come when I can find the right blend of exercise and rest, to add to my determination. I need a target, a date when I can show the world that Mutley is back, and I decide on Christmas. I will be there when Nigel's friends join him for his day. Everyone tells me I am not a good patient, and I know the only way I can make us all happy is not to be a patient at all.

Tim has stopped going to the hospital and seems more relaxed. The fire in his living room burns all day, every day, and I love lying by it; the warmth is reassuring. I feel it giving me strength and want to see the same in Tim, but his face stays pale, and his eyes have stopped talking to me. We sit so we can feel the warmth of the fire, but also see the view of the garden through the large French windows. The sun is out, but it's still bleak and I can sense the chill in the breeze as it ruffles the garden hedge.

I am looking at it, for no particular reason, when a beautiful and very large cock pheasant emerges. It is dark, almost black, and walks with great pride. I am on my feet, and so close to the glass that my breath mists it. In that moment, I know I will work again. If the window had been open, I would have been onto the bird in seconds. As it is, I jump where I am, hopping up and down. In my heart I am in one of the high woods and the valley is below. I look to Tim, and he is excited too, but when I look back the bird has gone. Was it really there, or was I dreaming? It doesn't matter, it is our reactions that matter – I am alive again, and so is Tim!

The pheasants are being driven across the valley, so everyone is on duty, and I have a chance to slip away. I walk slowly up the rutted track, taking the easy route where Billy's vehicle has cleared the snow. The ground still glistens with frost, and I have no intention of hurting my leg. Before I arrive at the spot where I first saw the body, I drop down into the valley. The wood runs right down to the river here, but a narrow path runs beside it, wandering between the old trees. Then the woodland opens out, and the expanse of rushes and flooded meadow lead to the spot I am heading for, the area downstream of the body. I pick my way; I know it well. I have retrieved many birds from here, high flying birds that couldn't make it to the woods beyond. Eventually, I arrive at the spot where I believe Kate found the bag and look about.

If I were a man, carrying a gun and a cartridge bag, and I wanted to get to the spot where I found the body - and do so quickly, through the driving snow - what would I do? I think of the bag. Yes, it had been heavy, filled with unused cartridges. I remember how Kate had struggled with it, and how I had too, as I carried it to my cedar tree. If I had been a man, I would have dropped it so I could walk faster, of course I would. The gun could be loaded, and I could hurry on. Part of me, my subconscious part, wants to look for scents but I know no relevant scents could still be here.

I push on and come to the spot I will never forget. In my mind the body is before me, and I focus on it. Did it have a wound, had the man been shot? No, he hadn't, and the police agreed. But he did have a wound, didn't he, just as if he had been hit by something hard, like a gun butt. All I need to do now is work out who walked the way I walked, greeted a fellow sportsman, then killed him and calmly drifted away.

When I think of sportsmen, I think of his fellow guests. I hadn't considered them, as I had assumed my body was to do with Joe's death. Have I been walking up the wrong path? Were the deaths and the tweeds a coincidence?

As I return to the castle, I am happier. I am sure I know how the murder was committed, but am I any nearer finding the murderer? Who would have walked as I did? Who would have known the way? The beaters would, as would the team who worked the picking up dogs. Regular guests would, as would Billy, Fred and Nigel – and the man's fellow guests? The smile leaves my face as I realise that I may know how it happened but am no nearer to actually identifying the killer.

No one seems to have missed me and very little interrupts the rest of my day. That is, until Billy's Land Rover returns from the valley, drops off Sarah and heads on to sort the day's bag. The guests follow in their three cars; cars that came clean but are now splattered with mud. They spill wet dogs and spent cartridges onto the gravel drive, before carrying their guns into the castle and upstairs, into the gun room. I hear Nigel's Land Rover drawing up outside and I run to it. They were delayed looking for a bird and have clearly found it by the way Nigel congratulates Kate before rushing in to join the guests.

I expect Kate to be cheerful. There is little more satisfying than a good retrieve, especially late in the day, when you are tired, and the night is ready to move in; but she is not. Her face is a mask of worry. She rushes up to me and drags me through the open door, into the deserted office.

'It's growing, I knew it would, as soon as my back was turned.'

She walks to the corner and stands under the desk where it is darker, as if the darkness can kill the worry that haunts her.

'What's growing?', I ask, rather guiltily. Clearly, she thinks I should know what she's talking about. 'Remember, you are the one who sees things, not me!'

'That cloud, that wretched cloud'. I can tell she is now sitting, though the light has totally gone, and the room is in darkness.

I had left her to sort her 'cloud' alone, too wrapped up in my own self-pity?

'It was during the third drive, you know, the one where they bring the little burn downstream.' I nod, and she continues.

'It always takes a while, and we were waiting behind the second peg. We were well sheltered, and the sun had begun to shine, when suddenly it hit me! The cloud came from this cloudless sky and shrieked at me, so much so that I expected imminent disaster until I realised it was the same cloud I had seen before, but now much more powerful and threatening.' She crawls out from under the table, as if the worst of her tale is over. The telling of it has been a release valve, and she looks at me.

'So, what does it mean and when will it be?' I try to sound understanding and sympathetic. Even in the darkness I can sense worry. 'Is it Tim? It can't be Tim; I was with him yesterday and he's much better.' Tears well in my eyes as my thoughts drift to that glorious black pheasant.

The door opens a little, light streams in and Kate creeps quietly away, without replying to me. I had been hoping to share my latest thoughts on the murder, but see she is in no state to contribute. Perhaps I should carry on alone, at least till she has this 'cloud' business sorted.

Subtle changes take place in the castle. The girls rush gleefully around, go up and down short ladders, and hang lengths of bunting that remind me of the ground by my tree camp after a windy night. Peter and Nigel put small fir trees into buckets and carry them indoors, trying not to make a mess. All this means that Christmas is coming, a busy time! Small weddings chat around the fire; parties make a noise in the marquee and, of course, there are more sporting groups.

I try to ignore them. I meet them when they are at the castle and hear how their days have gone. I try to sound excited and pleased that they have enjoyed their days, and my sadness at missing out turns to determination.

Peter is across the lawn, hanging coloured lights around the lake, and I know he will soon do the same on the tree by the castle door. All this normally happens when I am away working – which is where I should be now!

Kate is nowhere to be seen, despite the fact that there is no group here today. She was up before I woke this morning and is hiding somewhere in the castle. I have looked in the obvious places - under the cedar tree, at Tim's, by the rabbit burrows under the big beech tree - but she is at none of them. I decide I have searched enough. Serious though the 'cloud' is to her, there is little I can do if she won't speak to me.

Iona has come for her aunt's wedding. She is small, seven or eight, and has large, dark blue eyes. She is with her parents, younger brothers and small terrier called Bert. Bert is a moody dog and the only terrier I've ever met who has not been interested in either my rabbits or their holes. And he doesn't like children, which is a pity, as he shares his life with three of them. Anyway, I think this is why Iona is a little unsure of me at first. She is standing outside her room in the stable yard, waiting for her mother. I want to encourage her onto the lawn; to show her how lovable I am. It seems so long since the high-pitched, happy voice of a child called to me as we ran over to my camp below the pine tree. I have missed it and need it more than ever, but Iona does not want to play. The sun is beginning to set and soon it will be dark and cold.

I make my way towards the cottage and realise I have forgotten about my leg! I ask myself how it feels; is it still numb, or does it ache? Is it good that I have forgotten, or just another sign of my increasing age? I make a short run and find the numbness is gone. I must do a little more each day so that I will be ready for my return.

I enter the cottage and see Kate hiding in her bed beside the Aga, so I go to my bed and lie down as if exhausted, waiting for her to speak. I want to ask her the many questions that have been queuing up but know that she will already know what they are. I'm sure she has only been avoiding me as she doesn't have the answers. Perhaps she does now?

'Don't ask me how I know, I just do; and yes, it is the old cloud, and it must involve Tim.' The directness and anger in her voice shocks me.

So many questions, but the only one that matters is 'when?' Before I can ask, she says,

'Soon, very soon.'

I snuggle my nose between my paws and close my eyes. I need to balance Kate's words with my memory of Tim looking at the big cock pheasant, a look with so much life.

In the morning, we have more snow, which settles and starts to blow across the road. A conference arrives, and everyone gathers by the roaring fire. They talk to themselves less than usual and I decide it is not a real conference and more a party. I leave them to it and make my way to Tim's cottage. My path under the fence is covered with snow, so I scratch it clear and slip through.

Tim is in his bed, propped up with pillows. I look into his eyes and see that his body is much weaker. I know Kate is right, but I go on talking, sure he can hear me. Eventually the fire dies down and Tim is asleep. The day has passed so quickly; now evening is drawing in and, although the room is warm, I can sense how cold it is outside. Sarah returns from wherever she has been, and I make my way back across the lawn.

The frozen snow crackles as I walk. Thoughts of my trip up the valley interrupt my sadness and I let them take over. I scratch away the snow that has crept under my cedar tree and snuggle down. I want to sleep but know I need answers. There is little point in knowing how the killer worked his evil magic if the 'how' doesn't tell me who he was. And was it even a man?

I know nothing of the group that day, or their dogs, and they didn't stay here at the castle. Even if I have been down the wrong road, I decide to keep going, for now at least. So, it was a man who wanted to kill Joe. What do I know about Joe? He was a good man. A man who loved Kate and whom Kate loved, but there must be more. There was a secret shared with Ian, but was that the only one? Did Joe know Hamish? Something tells me he did. I have never been patient. I must trust my senses as Kate does her 'clouds'. The snow begins to fall heavily again, so I return to the castle, its coloured lights appearing as bright smudges in the growing gloom.

The snow is so deep the conference can't leave, so they stay another night. I slip out again, spend time with Tim, and return tired and sad. Every day he seems weaker, and his eyes need to work harder to talk with me. I walk through the snow up to the lake and towards my tree camp, but everything is hidden. The waterfall is still flowing and when the snow is blown onto it, it sits for just a second before disappearing. I walk on into the trees above the lake. The snow is lighter here and I expect to see rabbit tracks, but there are none. Again, nothing is as it should be, as I need it to be!

It's well into the afternoon before the conference folk leave. Billy came to tell us that the road was open, and the small convoy made their way home, with Billy and Nigel escorting them in their old Land Rovers. The sun appears briefly, then dies as the darkness comes and the cold grows. The coloured lights by the lake shine on the snow and glisten on the ice. Nigel and Billy are returning, the sound echoing up the valley long before they appear. Kate is by my side, looking up into the sky, and I see she is about to speak. I prepare for another vision, but she simply smiles and says,

'Well, if those guys can get out, the sporting guests should get in', and runs off to meet Nigel and Billy.

So that's why they were in such a hurry to get the conference guests away!

The sportsmen arrive late and, by the time he has given them a night cap, Nigel doesn't make his way past my bed till the early hours. The night is especially quiet and seems to go on for ever, but then I hear Nigel moving and join him to feed the cattle. Oliver is still away, and no one asks when he will be back.

When we return to the castle, the last of the party have just gone through for breakfast; they will struggle to be on time! The phone rings and Nigel bustles past me to answer it. As he returns, he stops and bends down,

'How are you feeling, how's the leg?'

I am very surprised and leap excitedly to my feet, looking as much like a super fit dog as I can.

'Well, we are several dogs short today, if you feel up to it.'

I run around the room like a puppy, bouncing with happiness. Where is Kate - I must tell her the news!

Old times are here again, and we lurch our way from the castle in the Land Rover, sitting on the old sack. Kate stands and tries to make out where we are going, but I have suffered these bumps often enough to know we are headed for the top wood. Nigel and Billy help a guest who is struggling up the hill, and we wait.

'You were good not to push me for more details about Tim', says Kate, rubbing the dirty window with her nose. 'I thought you might argue with me.'

'No, you are right; Tim will not be with us much longer, though I don't like admitting it. But if you can now be rid of 'clouds' and get back to your old self again, at least some good will have resulted.'

The rear door opens with a flourish of cold air, and we are away. My first day back will be a success, I know, and I look across at Kate with the confidence of a dog who has found the bone he had lost.

However, it turns out to be a strange day. The birds still don't like the snow and are reluctant to fly; and when they do, they are easily dazzled by the slightest flash of sun. Kate works with Billy and Nigel takes me along the track to where the burn crosses it at a small ford. Several birds follow the tree line above us and fall into the bank in front.

At first, Nigel hesitates to let me work, especially where the snow has drifted, but soon he sees I'm fine and three birds are safely lying by his feet. At lunch, the bag is small, but the guests seem happy enough, and the sound of eating, drinking and merrymaking echoes across the yard. Something catches my eye as I pass a vehicle. It is only a coat, but part of the tweed is the orange that only one person would wear!

Bill is in Billy's Land Rover, hiding below the driver's seat, and I go to cheer him. This is where I usually find him when Billy is being hard work, and Kate has already told me that he's in a foul mood today.

'How is Ben?', I ask. Although I haven't seen him for a while, I'm told he has worked well while I've been resting. Bill looks up from his sadness.

'He's OK, though Billy still can't wait to get rid of him.'

'Why?', I ask. 'I thought he was doing well.'

'He is, but you know Billy', Bill replies. 'Ask him yourself', he adds, looking towards a low hovel in the corner. Ben is lying there, with a length of rusty chain preventing him joining the rest of the dogs. What can he have done to deserve such isolation?

'Is Hamish here, you know, the man with the awful orange tweed?', I add.

'Oh yes, he's here. Why do you think Billy's in such a mood!'

I'll find out more from Nigel later, but for now I need Ben to answer a question. I go over to him and, after a few minutes small talk, I come to it.

'Think back Ben, to that awful day when your master died. How did you get down to the valley with it snowing so hard?'

'Oh, we drove. We just made it to the bridge where the water from the loch joins the river and walked downstream.'

This is new; no one has told me of a vehicle being found there; it must be where the police think the body floated from. Something else to ask Nigel!

'With it snowing so hard, why did you go? It seems a lot of effort for one bird.'

My words are bringing back bad memories for Ben. He has suffered under Billy, and I am adding to them. I don't think he will answer, but then he looks at me with determined eyes.

'I agree, but my master was keen to go, and Billy had told him where to look. It was as if he was on a mission!'

What sort of mission could be worth going out in such a blizzard, I ask myself? The questions just keep mounting.

19

It comes in the middle of the night. The unmistakable sound of an ambulance in a hurry, echoing eerily against the snowy background. I am uneasy all night and find sleep impossible. I know immediately what it means. Nigel leaves in a hurry, his face a mixture of tiredness and sadness, and his mind too distant to speak. All I can do is stand at my French windows with Kate beside me and wish Tim well.

I remember all the things I should have told him but haven't, and our plans for Christmas, which seems so far away. I visited him last night, ready to recount the details of the day while they were fresh in my mind, but he was asleep. I looked around his room and wondered then whether I would see him again.

And now it has been confirmed; Tim died last night. The ambulance that came in a great hurry sat idly for ages, and when it did leave, did so very quietly. I'm scared to go to the castle this morning and don't want to look into Tim's garden. I remember how sad Nigel was when old Gunner died. I watched as he buried him in the lawn by the edge of the drive, so the old dog could watch for the postman coming. I remember how he had planted the tree, with leaves that are red in the autumn and branches that drooped over him to keep him cool in the summer. It's the tree the rabbits tried to kill and, as you know, sometimes I lie there and think of him. Old friends seem important when I'm sad! At last, I build up the courage to crawl under the fence. Sarah is there, sitting in her chair but everything else is quiet, so I go to her. I sit beside her, as I did for Tim, and she strokes me.

Later, she comes to the castle and talks with Nigel. I haven't seen them together since Gwen left and wonder what will happen now. I move outside to the lawn; I am happier here when I don't know what to do. The clouds are drifting lazily across the sky as if they are somehow caught in the sadness of Tim's death and don't quite know where to go. I try to smell the weather, but the ability has left me.

From my sheltered spot under the cedar tree, I can see Tim's house. I see its roof, and the way it stands clear of the tall box hedge, but it is no longer the same house.

A good friend - one of my best - has gone, and now life must move on. Kate has seemed much happier since I accepted the truth about Tim, and I look forward to the return of the old confident Kate that I knew; the Kate who could rule the world with Joe by her side.

As I enter the castle, I sense something is wrong. Kate is in the office, curled up in the corner on Nigel's old armchair, and she's shaking.

'It hasn't gone', she croaks, as if the very mention of her 'cloud' causes her actual pain. 'It's still here, and it's growing even stronger. You know what that means, don't you?'

I try to think. This is not how it was meant to be. If the 'cloud' did not foretell the death of Tim, what did it mean? I lie down beside Kate's chair, but neither of us can think of anything to say.

All too quickly, it is the day of Tim's funeral. Nigel pinned a note to the castle door saying simply, 'CLOSED', before leaving with the girls, Peter and Billy a few minutes ago. Kate and I are holding the fort. Earlier, Sarah had insisted on us having a bath, and for once we didn't argue.

'If you want to join us for tea, you must look the part', she had insisted, covering me in a rich, soapy lather.

I think of the day I was a bridesmaid back in the summer; the lather is the same but everything else is so different. As the last car leaves for the church, a unique silence falls on the castle and everything around it. Kate walks to the cedar tree, and I join her there. We lie down carefully. I have never been so clean and, for once, I want to stay that way. Kate closes her eyes and, for a while, we just listen to the breeze murmuring through the trees. I sit up; it is time for Kate and I to refocus. I look at her.

'The body walked to where I found him, after parking his vehicle next to the loch bridge.' I wonder if my sharp words will earn a response; anything to take us away from today!

'What, when did you find this out?', she asks, with more energy than I could have hoped for.

'At the last day up the valley. I asked Ben, and he told me. I realised it was snowing too hard for someone to drive down the grass field.'

Kate sits up too, her mind working overtime. 'What happened to the car?'

'The police took it away, or so Nigel told me this morning.'

'Typical', she barks, and leaps to her feet. 'Why didn't he say before? So, now we know the man walked to his death, and do we think the murderer walked there too?'

'Yes', I reply. 'I don't think a vehicle could have driven out of the field with the snow as it was.'

Kate nods. 'So, we have to find some other use for the tracks.'

🐾

The wake goes as well as it could; Sarah gaining strength from Nigel, and he from her. Oliver's absence is felt, and when Sarah leaves later to be with him, I think how hard it must be for her to lose her son, knowing she is about to lose her husband too.

🐾

Kate is suffering as well. The 'cloud' has given her a troubled night, and she doesn't leave her bed till nearly midday.

In the afternoon, an old man with white hair and a worn tweed jacket comes to the door; his name is Fred. He's followed by one of the cheeriest groups we have hosted all season. Fred's wife never stops talking and the whitest Spaniel sits at her heel. Suddenly, I see that among the party are Richard and his beautiful Spaniel, Bess, and I want to be with them. I want to show Bess that I am a genuine, hardworking, happy dog - despite Kate's snide remarks in the summer!

All the party are characters, either very tall, or very fat, or very old, and they have all known each other for years. When they move to the bar, I hear Nigel laughing for the first time since Tim died. Sarah sits in the corner, leaning on the bar and smiling too, her eyes fixed firmly on Nigel. As Kate and I entertain Bess and Fred's dog, whose name is Benny, I know this is just the party we all need.

We are all late to bed and, considering how much is weighing on our minds - or on Kate's, at least - we sleep well. Again, I join Nigel for the morning check on the cattle and sheep; and have begun to look upon it as a very important time with him. It has been a cold night, and the cattle are all on the hill, enjoying the early sunshine. I trot down to see them, keeping well clear of the cows, and carry on to the bottom, enjoying a cool, fresh drink from the burn. Two families of rabbits live in the hedge, and I scent them, but my mind is elsewhere today. Kate and her 'cloud' haunt me. I return to find Nigel leaning on the old vehicle. He looks at me, shading his eyes from the rising sun and relaxing. Happiness is returning. The ground is very rough and frozen and I'm afraid he thinks I'm limping, so I run the last bit, jumping over a patch of old straw and bouncing by him like a puppy.

'OK, Mutley, I know you're much better, you don't have to prove it!'

I hop onto his seat and look proudly across the valley.

Last evening has certainly perked him up. Was it the guests, Sarah, or both? Should I mention Kate's 'cloud'? I decide that, even in his present good mood, he would struggle to understand, and it's not mine to share anyway.

Everyone, including Billy and Bill, is waiting at the castle. The group is here for two days of 'tidy up' shooting and we dogs are raring to go. Billy is not so happy; he prefers straightforward days in the main woods. By lunchtime we know they are probably the worst shots this year. I am near Fred all morning and he takes more shots than anyone, but bags only two birds, both of which Benny retrieves with great relish.

I look at Benny as he comes with the second bird. As I've told you, he is very white, with just a large spot on one ear and a smudge beside his tail. The snow remains where it's drifted and, for a second, he totally merges with the whiteness so that it seems as though a single black spot is carrying the bird!

The second day is like the first. The sun shines and Billy finds lots of birds, most of which fly on. As Fred, Benny and the rest of the party leave in convoy, another car enters the drive. It's the first of tomorrow's wedding party and carries three lively children.

Nigel welcomes the parents and looks at me. 'Do you want to show the boys your tree camp, Mutley?'

I shoot him a confident look. 'Certainly boss; it's a little snowy but ready for inspection.'

The wedding goes as well as it could, considering the loss of Tim still fills our hearts and our heads. I learn we are to have no more weddings or sporting days till after Christmas, and then it's just the family day before the end of year celebrations. Plenty of time then to sort out this 'cloud' business!

When I wake, I see Nigel is already away, and rush out to find him. His Land Rover is still in the drive, so I dive under the cottage fence; he must be with Sarah. He's not there, and nor is she; they must be in the castle after all. I find them in the office, talking about Oliver. Sarah has just returned from seeing him and I learn that he is dying and does not have long left. Poor Sarah!

Kate is curled up in Nigel's chair. Has she told them about her 'cloud', or is she telling them she has some other problem? She seems to perk up when I arrive, rolls out of the chair and walks slowly into the garden. I follow her to the cedar tree.

The lawn is white and frozen, but here, under the tree, the ground is its usual brown, with fir needles and a reassuring warmth. I snuggle beside Kate and wait for her to talk, but after a while I can wait no longer.

'So, if the cloud did not see the end of Tim, what did it see? Is it for the end of Oliver, is that the message?'

She remains silent! I begin to wonder if she is in shock. Eventually she starts to speak, though without the confidence I want.

'It could be Oliver, but I won't know till his end comes, which Sarah says won't be long.'

'But you don't think its Oliver, do you? Is that what's worrying you? If it's not Oliver, could it be something bigger than either Tim or Oliver, something bigger than you want to consider?'

She buries her nose between her paws and lets out a quiet whimper, one I have never heard before. For several minutes we just lie there. It's as if the words have drained all her energy. Then she gets slowly to her feet and wanders, dream-like, to the cottage. I follow a few yards behind.

20

Kate has gone out with Joe's friend, Chris, and I am pleased. She still hasn't told me more about her 'cloud', and sometimes I wonder if she ever will. Christmas Day is one of our busiest days and we rush around getting ready. Some guests will be staying, and some will just come for their lunch. Either way, they will want to be pampered, and I am an expert at that. There will be children and, again, I know what to do.

Kate returns late in the day, and I find her where I expect to, in Nigel's office chair. Is she's waiting for me? She certainly isn't surprised when I rush in.

'You look better, do you feel better?', I ask. My heart is beating faster than ever. I want instant answers, but sense she wants to take her time.

'I'm trying to live with the cloud; I must, it's the only way I can beat it. It's growing, and my only hope is that by staying with it I can understand it.'

My questions become irrelevant. As I look at her, I see she's in actual pain. I want to cuddle her, but sense she needs my strength now; the sensitive me can come later.

'Do you have any clues where it's taking us, any at all?'

I think she's going to snap at me, to relieve the pressure if nothing else, but she doesn't. After a deep breath, she goes on.

'No, I'm trying to be logical, to analyse what could be so important that it's giving me such a strong warning.'

'Do you think it's a warning? Does that mean we have the chance to stop something, or at least make it less serious?'

This is new; it's the first time she has suggested we could influence the events of which her 'cloud' foretells. I am excited and want to go on, but she stops me.

'I don't know, but it's our only hope. We must think what it could be. It is big, Mutley, so big that without the hope of solving it, I think it could take me with it.'

The thought of this shocks me into silence till voices sound from the hallway. Nigel and Chris are coming. We break our spell and enter the present. Nigel sees Chris to his car, where Kate says her farewell, then Nigel jumps into his Land Rover and calls me - he is late with his round of the stock. As we race up the drive, I see Kate turn, making for the office. I wish her well with her thinking; so much may depend on it!

The next morning, Nigel and I are up and off early. The sky is angry, and the sun seems a long way off. Nigel is trying to get ahead, as it's Christmas Eve tomorrow. We have driven to the far end of the loch, beyond the boathouse and the crab apple trees to the long, flat meadow that lies below the high, scree-covered slopes. Nigel has walked over the frozen ground to the far end of the meadow and is feeding the stock some hay. I am waiting for him by the loch side. The sun is shining, and I hear the water lapping gently onto the shore. Downstream, the boathouse looks calm and welcoming, and beyond it the fir woods show as vivid green in the whiteness, where the early sun is catching them.

Nigel blows his horn. I have been dreaming, but as I turn to hop up beside him a streak of darkness swoops over me. It makes me miss my step and I need to take a second jump to reach my seat.

'Are you alright?', Nigel asks with sudden concern.

'Fine', I lie.

I am anything but fine. Is this 'cloud', whatever it is, getting to me now too? I snuggle down in my seat and hope Kate will have some news for me. As we drive in, I spy her under the cedar tree. We pull up, Nigel rushes indoors - so many jobs and so little time - and I run over to join Kate. I tell her of my experience by the lake, and she just nods.

'It's as I feared, as it grows stronger even those with lesser gifts will start to feel it.' She can see I am shaken and tries to reassure me.

'We must list the events that are set to happen soon and all those involved. Once we have done that, hopefully something will stand out.'

As we think and list, we realise what a bad time the 'cloud' has chosen:

'Well, there's Christmas and all that goes with it, the friends' sporting party and their stay, and then the New Year Celebrations, or is that too far off?'

I look at Kate. Clearly, she has been through all this in her mind whilst I have been away and come to the same conclusion. She grimaces with pain, and I know the longer we leave it, the weaker she will become!

'I think we must plan for it being at Christmas and go from there', I say, as I look at Kate rubbing her paws up and down her nose.

The guests who are staying for Christmas arrive in the afternoon and we are hardly ready. All week the team have laboured to get things perfect and then, this morning, a leak appeared. The cold-water pipe in one of the bedrooms has burst and it's soaked the carpets, both there and in the chapel below. We don't need the chapel today or tomorrow, but we do need the bedroom tonight.

Within a few hours, the leak has been fixed, the carpet is drying, and the sound of fan heaters echoes through the building. Kate and I leap into disaster mode, checking for dangerous ceilings or rotten floors and generally annoy everyone. To the team, Nigel especially, we are a total pain and are soon banished to the cottage. We decide to be more measured in our reactions, for our own sakes as much as everyone else's. Christmas is always stressful, but with the death of Tim, Oliver's sickness and the 'cloud' taking on the dimensions of a thunderstorm, we are in unchartered territory.

The day draws into night and no new disasters have occurred. However, between my own worries and Kate's moaning, it's almost impossible for me to get any sleep. At this rate, we will both have to stay in bed tomorrow!

Everyone seems to be coming for Christmas lunch. The same parties come every year, and the children grow bigger and noisier. All morning, the smell of turkey - one of my absolute favourite foods - drifts from the kitchen whenever someone opens the door, teasing me. More guests arrive, and I rush to them as if they are the most important party in the world, then run around till someone tells me to settle down, while everyone laughs.

Kate has stayed at the cottage, as I thought she would. This is a busy day and no place for a Christmas novice, especially one who's unwell. Later in the day she comes over for a few minutes, then, sensing no disasters, creeps away again.

The 'cloud' grows, and I brace myself for the next time it comes to me. It would be better if I could run outside, but it's raining. Slowly, the rooms become less crowded, and the noise dies down. Sarah is busy all day – the whole team is, especially now that Gwen and Ian have gone - and I wonder if it's better for her to be occupied; to have less time to brood and remember. When the door eventually closes on the last party, everyone sighs with relief. The tables in the bar are re-laid and the team start their own party, but I slip away and join Kate.

🐾

Morning comes, and we are all still alive! The rain has stopped, and all the residents are out walking, except one elderly couple who are still in bed. The fire is roaring downstairs, warming the drawing room for the guests' return.

The warmth drives me to sleep. I dozily watch the flames dancing and soon I'm dreaming. I'm in Tim's sitting room and he's in his chair. I can hear Sarah in the kitchen and smell the lunch cooking. Someone is missing from my dream; I realise it's Oliver and look for him. I hear a voice beside me, not in the room or the present, but beside me, as in another dream, and I know its Oliver, calling, warning. Why is he not in the first dream, I ask myself, and why is he calling? What is he warning us of?

I stir myself and move over to the big window, where I can watch for the guests' return. The friends' day up the valley can only be a day or two away, and Christmas has come and nearly gone. The guests bustle back in, eat their buffet lunch and then drive off to their homes, wherever that may be. Kate is spread out beside the fire, enjoying the warmth. For the first time in a while, she is truly asleep.

A whisper comes from the doorway, and I see Nigel gesturing to me. I walk quietly to join him and soon we are driving. Are we checking livestock or planning the friends' day? We are doing both, and as soon as we have counted the sheep in the long field, we head for the loch. We haven't been to the loch on a sporting day since very early in the season and I see he wants to do it.

Nigel is looking up to the thin tree line at the top of the hill, at the ridge below it and then down and along the loch side. The boathouse looks as it did a few days ago, welcoming, and I am still looking at it when I am knocked over and almost fall in the water. Nigel hasn't seen, he is still looking up the hill, but I am on the ground and shaking. There is nothing there, nothing real, and I know it's the 'cloud'. The sun dies, and everything becomes dark, darker than the darkest storm. Slowly I stand, my balance returns, and I climb into the vehicle. I curl up as if asleep and we bump our way back to the castle. Slowly the sun returns.

Kate is awake, but in great pain and has gone back to the cottage. I join her there and tell her of my frightening dark 'cloud'. Strangely, this seems to make her feel better; perhaps it's just knowing that someone is sharing it.

'Why do you think you saw both clouds by the loch? Is that relevant?', she asks.

'I don't think so. The first time we were checking cattle and the second we were planning the sporting day. And even though the location was roughly the same, we were at opposite ends of the loch. It doesn't really add up.'

'Perhaps, but we must beware whenever anyone is going near the loch; do you agree?'

'I do.'

She doesn't speak for a few seconds and when I look across, she is sleeping again. The smallest thing exhausts her.

🐾

Harry is first to arrive for the annual friends' day. It's just after lunch, and soon everyone is here. I learn there will be a short memorial service for Joe in the Chapel - so that was why they were drying it out yesterday! The service is short, just a few prayers and Joe's favourite hymn. Kate and I sit at the back and are glad to leave when Sarah opens the door; chapels are strange places! We sit under the chestnut tree just outside and watch as everyone moves from the chapel to the bar. Harry is with Andy, two of Joe's oldest friends, and they are followed by David and Richard, who missed last year. Nigel closes the chapel door and follows, his arm around Sarah. Everyone is so happy, even in sadness. I hope nothing happens to change that!

A new world greets us in the morning. Snow has swept in overnight and is already several inches deep. At breakfast, everyone keeps looking out, unable to believe the weather could change so fast, and Billy is wondering what they should do. He and Nigel chat in the corner while everyone pretends to ignore them and drink their coffee. Suddenly Billy leaves - something has been agreed - and Nigel returns, his mood transformed.

'Come on boys, we need to get a move on.'

Everyone puts down their cups, swallows the last forkful of bacon and rushes away; voices cheery and hearts lightened. Kate is determined to join us, though we both know she can barely stand, let alone walk, and I spend my time trying to find out the order of the day.

The ache in my leg has been replaced with a numbness, but not the numbness I know. As I have told you, I always feel excited before a sporting day, when I will have to call on my instincts and knowledge to find the birds, but today is different. The excitement is there, but something wants to overtake it. Is this the 'cloud'? Is it so close that even I can't escape it? I look at Kate, but her eyes are shut tight.

Soon we are in the Land Rover and heading for the lunch hut. The snow drifts across the road and the hill seems lost in it. Snow again; the thought of it makes me shiver! Will it always? The guests unload, chatting cheerfully as they peer through the blizzard and laugh. Soon they are all in the hut. I want to go in and find out more information about the day, but I dare not leave Kate. Should I tell her how I feel - how the 'cloud' is affecting me? I can see her determination fighting through the pain, but am not sure which will win. I can see she has done all she can, it's up to me now!

Eventually Bill comes out and I ask him what we are doing.

'We are having three drives this morning and, hopefully, two this afternoon', he answers, as he hurries towards Billy's Land Rover. Billy seems in an unusually good mood today, and Bill won't want to spoil it.

'Are any near the loch?', I call, but he just shrugs his shoulders and flops his ears that are wet with snow.

I decide the snow will have scuppered the loch idea. The loch drive needs sun. I feel a small wave of relief.

We start just behind the lunch barn, and I persuade Kate to rest there while we do it. It's a small wood and any birds that are there will drift across the field below and can easily be dealt with by the other dogs. Only half a dozen pheasants appear, though I'm sure more will have been tucked up in the bushes, hiding from the snow, which continues to fall. It is blowing across the open field and adding to my numbness. The team appears out of the whiteness, and Bill, his black coat a smudge in the snow, is leading the way.

Kate has moved to the yard and is breathing deeply, trying to regain as much energy as she can. She knows we have finished in the small wood and are ready to move on. Billy walks past the spot where she has been sheltering beside the wall, puts some birds in the game trailer and turns. Kate hears him turn and looks up at him. As she does, Billy looks her directly in the eye and she stumbles. Billy leaps into the Land Rover, speeds away and Kate is left panting!

Andy, Billy's assistant, is talking to the guests.

'We will be heading for a spot up the valley, where a small cottage sits. It's at the end of the top road.' He points through the snow into the distance. Then he looks at Kate and me and adds, 'Nigel asked for you two to help me; the birds will take a lot of moving in weather like this.'

I know it. In the summer, it's a lovely, sheltered spot, and today it will be too, out of the wind. As the snow falls with renewed vigour, I think Nigel has picked the right place. Many birds will have taken refuge there, away from the cold wind.

Andy continues. 'Seven guests will be at the front, for those birds that fly down the valley, and two at the back, for those heading for the loch.'

As soon as I hear the word 'loch', a shiver runs through me and when I look about, I can't see Nigel. I look again and can't see Billy either.

Andy, the young keeper, is now in the Land Rover. 'Where are Nigel and Billy?', I want to ask, and then I hear Harry doing just that.

'Oh, they are taking the back track', Andy replies. 'Nigel needs to get to the back peg and Billy is bringing in the flank. It's the best way in weather like this.'

I know full well that this back track goes past the loch! Kate appears by my feet. She has been trying to say something, but my mind is elsewhere.

'Andy will have to manage without us', I shout to Kate, as we race off into the wood.

The wood is a different world; the wind becomes a distant hush and only the odd flake makes its way through the fir canopy. I make good time, but Kate is struggling and shouts for me to leave her. I know she will come as fast as she can; I just hope she remembers the way! At the bottom, I meet the road and see the fresh tracks the vehicles have left. I hop into one and bound after the boys. The wind is still quiet, interrupted by the trees, but the snow is falling here, which makes the track slippery, and again I feel panic growing in me. When I round the corner, I expect to see the vehicles as they make their way between the wood and the loch, but there is nothing. I stop and listen, but can only hear the wind, my beating heart and my lungs gulping for breath.

Suddenly, I see a slight movement at the edge of the loch and race to it. For a second, I'm frozen with horror. Billy's Land Rover is at the edge of the water, and Nigel's is out there, slowly sinking. Billy is standing, smiling and watching the bubbles rise as the vehicle sinks. Why isn't he jumping in? I leap past him and swim the dozen or so yards that the truck has floated, arriving at the driver door just as Nigel is trying to open it. Someone is already there, helping. I push my head through the gap and wait for Nigel's hand to grasp me. I then pull back and slowly help him to the shore, where Kate has just arrived, her eyes glazed with panic and effort. She jumps past me and, as I turn, I see the man who was there to help. It is Oliver!

'I have him!', someone shouts, grasping Nigel by the shoulder and I turn and swim to join Kate. It's hard work, Oliver has become a dead weight. We nose him above the water, Harry and Richard join us, and we finally get him back onto the land.

Billy's Land Rover bursts into life. As he races along the bottom road, he picks up his phone. 'Sorry Sis, it's all gone wrong, it's time to make a move.'

Many miles away, Gwen turns to Ian and lowers her mobile.

21

'Didn't you see I wanted to warn you, to tell you that it was Billy who ran Joe and I off the road?', Kate says between deep breaths. She is exhausted, but relief is giving her energy.

'When he looked me in the eye in the yard, I realised they were the same eyes I saw that night. He had always been careful to look away before.'

I snuggle up to her, the time for the sensitive me has come. Exhaustion wants to take over again, but curiosity is too strong for Kate.

'But Billy had so much to lose', Kate says, looking at me and shaking her head.

An ambulance has arrived, the paramedics have fought their way through the snow, and they are leaning over Oliver. I see one look at another and shake his head. Nigel is sitting up, a towel around his shoulders. His face is full of confusion, but he is in good hands now.

I look along the track that borders the loch. It is filling with guests, beaters and worried-looking policemen trying to take control. Where has Billy gone? Have they stopped him? Kate's voice brings me back to her.

'And why didn't we know Billy and Gwen were brother and sister?'

I can only shrug an answer.

A policeman has taken a towel from the ambulance and is drying Kate. She is shivering, and her head is resting between her paws. But when her eyes meet mine, I know the pressure is lifting and that she will be alright. I take a breath and realise someone is drying me too. When they finish, I turn towards Kate.

'I think Gwen had convinced Billy that Joe had overheard them discussing how they would take over the estate.' Kate nods, though mention of Joe's name makes her look away.

'Did he really believe that Nigel would end the sporting days when Oliver died?'

I look at Kate. 'I don't know, Billy had become a troubled soul, who knows what he believed?'

Kate nods again, sadly. 'And had he? Had Joe actually overheard their plans?' She looks at me with tears in her eyes. What does she want me to say?

'We will never know, but I doubt it. If he had known of their plans, he would have told Nigel, wouldn't he? I think Gwen had promised Billy that after Oliver and Nigel had died, she would inherit the whole estate, and the sporting days would become his.'

'And he believed it was worth all those deaths to achieve?' Kate shakes her head again.

'Gwen could be very convincing, you know.'

Kate gives a wry smile, but then another thought breaks through her exhaustion.

'But surely Billy would have recognised Joe, and he would have known he wasn't with them that day.'

It's my turn to smile.

'You would think so, but Gwen had given him the cap to make sure he got things right, and it confused him. Billy was not a natural killer. He panicked!'

'But why?'

'I think it was the snow, it nearly spoilt everything. Remember, a blizzard raced in at the end of the day, and everyone rushed home. Billy saw the man in the tweed about to go and felt he needed to stop him, confusing the tweed with Joe - and, by the way, the man's name was Tony. So, Billy told Tony that his highest bird had collapsed and fallen next to the old oak tree. And no one wants to leave their highest bird, the high point of their day!'

Kate nods and smiles; the vanity of men!

'Billy told him to go on down and that he would join him there, so Tony and Ben did just that, while Billy walked upstream to intercept them. Then, murder committed, Billy retraced his steps, wearing Hamish's cap to confuse things.'

Kate smiles through her pain, but then another question forms. 'And the pheasant in Tony's hand, had Billy put it there?'

'Well, at first I thought it was some kind of joke, but then I knew that if Billy had wanted the police to believe it was an accident, the pheasant in the hand would confuse things. It's so unlikely that a body could float downstream and keep hold of a bird. No, I believe it was just another of Billy's errors. Tony must have had the bird in his hand when Billy struck. Then the reality of what he had done, and the sight of the body spooked him, and he rushed away. When he remembered he had left the gun, he had to return to get it – and that's when he should have taken the bird too. But, for whatever reason, he didn't.'

Kate closes her eyes. Someone has started an engine, and a rope leads from the shore to Nigel's Land Rover, which now has only its roof showing above the water. We move across the track and lie under a bush.

'And Jane, why did she have to die?' Kate looks at me.

'Jane undoubtedly found a letter addressed to Gwen from Hamish, probably outlining how the estate would be split up if Nigel and Oliver died. Remember, Hamish is a lawyer. I'm sure Jane realised something was wrong, but I don't think she knew much. She must have mentioned it as they cleared the summer house after the play on the lawn and, again, Billy panicked.'

Kate closes her eyes. She has accepted my summary for now, though I'm sure she will have more questions when her energy returns.

'Come on, boy', a policeman says to me as he opens his car door. A blanket has been laid across the rear seat and he gestures me to jump in. I hop up, but Kate staggers and needs to be lifted. A crackle comes over the police radio.

'You've stopped him, well done, I didn't think he would get far.' Billy has been caught! The policemen look at each other and smile, then turn towards me.

'We've taken your master to hospital, just for a check-up. No need to worry, I'm sure he'll be absolutely fine.'

They drive carefully, and I see the snow has stopped. The windows want to steam up, and I hear the fans working hard.

Kate looks up and I see she has more to say.

'So, have we been unfair to Hamish? Is he just an innocent buffoon?'

I smile and think of the times Hamish has annoyed me this year. His speech, and the bottle he gave to Billy that he thought made him appear so kind. The way he arrived for their partridge day, throwing dust and demanding coffee, and the look on Ben's face when he thought Hamish was the murderer. All these made him very annoying, but not a killer!

'Yes, he was Nigel's solicitor', I reply. 'I heard him telling Sarah after Gwen left and he was very full of himself. Buffoon is about right.'

'And his cartridge bag and cap had been left after their pre-Christmas shoot. It was so recognisable that Billy thought it would confuse things if he took it?', Kate ventures.

'Yes', I reply, 'although I think it may have been Gwen's idea; she had no love for Hamish.'

'And Billy returned the cap before this season, so everyone would see Hamish wearing it. And Nigel's whistle, Billy again, more confusion?'

Kate and I smile at each other as she releases her thoughts; at last things fit together. But then the smile disappears from Kate's face, as her mind goes back to Joe. I continue,

'Joe's death was silly Billy again. He had been told off by Ian and Gwen for killing Tony, even though they were pretty sure the police were convinced it had been an accident. But Billy felt he needed to prove himself. Somehow, he found out where Joe was having dinner that fateful night, drove there and killed him.'

Kate closes her eyes, but my mind can't switch off quite yet. It returns to Oliver. Was he really there, diving into the lake to save Nigel? I almost can't believe how he gathered his strength for that final act, the parting gift of a loving brother. I always knew he was a good man, but now he is a true hero.

I smile a sad smile and look at Kate. She desperately needs rest, but before I allow it, I ask for one assurance.

'No more 'clouds', please, no more.'

Her only response is a slight flicker of her long lashes.

I walk from the cottage the back way, past the big rhododendron. I want to flush a rabbit, but none are there, so I go on to my camp, which is full of snow. It will need a good clean out before I can show it to the next lot of children, but that can wait. I turn away and walk across the lawn towards the castle. In the distance, I hear the sound of Nigel's new Land Rover, and then I see it, driving up the valley.

Everything is back to normal, and yet nothing will be quite the same. Kate is still resting, and Bill and Ben are with her. She nearly killed herself but won't admit it. At least it seems that she will be okay, and I know the four of us will have lots of adventures together.

Sarah is reorganising the cottage. She is moving in next week and Nigel can't stop smiling.

Back in the castle, I hop onto my sofa. Perhaps now I'll get some peace at last!

THE END